The Women of Biafra

Onyeka Nwelue, born in 1988, is a Nigerian scholar, filmmaker, jazz musician and publisher, who has published over 25 books.

Nwelue was an Academic Visitor to the University of Oxford and Visiting Scholar in the University of Cambridge. He was a Visiting Research Fellow at Ohio University. He was a Research Associate at the University of Johannesburg.

He is the director of Africa Center México.

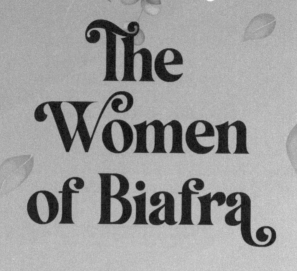

The Women of Biafra

Onyeka Nwelue

Abibiman
Publishing

New York & London

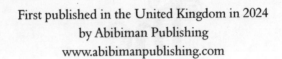

First published in the United Kingdom in 2024
by Abibiman Publishing
www.abibimanpublishing.com

ISBN: 978-1-0686383-0-5

Cover design by Fred Martins

Printed in Great Britain by Bell and Bain Ltd, Glasgow

Strangers of Braamfontein Review

"*Strangers of Braamfontein* is a perceptive and vigorous tale of people trapped in dire circumstances"

- *Kirkus Reviews*.

'*The Strangers of Braamfontein*' is heavily peopled with characters as dark as the night who are cohabiting in a brutal place where death is cheap. Raw, gritty, fast-paced, this is not a book you can glance through because it will force you to keep turning the pages. It will make you shiver with trepidation. It is such a searing read. This is a book to love.

- *Olukorede S. Yishau, The Lagos Review*.

"*The Strangers of Braamfontein* is one of those crime novels that hits you in the gut and before you can recover another powerful blow is delivered. It's a story of corruption, gangland violence, sex trafficking, modern slavery and murder. All of this is seen from the perspective of the people brutalised, abused and discarded and those profiting and perpetuating their misery."

- *Paul Burke, Crime Fiction Lover*.

"The novel features a colorful and sprawling cast of characters, each motivated by the dictates of a world where survival is in deed for the fittest."

- Alesia Alexander, Brittle Paper.

"There is no downtime with *The Strangers of Braamfontein*. The pacing is fast and is sustained all through to the last page. I like the character Osas, mostly. He represents the hopeful African youth who travels to break out of the dire situation at home. The drug lord Papi is another character I find very interesting, and then there is the prostitute who falls in love with Osas. This is my second time reading the book and I don't trust myself well enough to not come back to it repeatedly."

- Ikenna Okeh, Author of The Operative.

"Onyeka Nwelue's *The Strangers of Braamfontein* is timely and urgent, a necessary read, in view of recent happenings in South Africa. Moreover, it is a novel that African migration and diaspora scholars may find relevant in discussing intra-continental migration and its complexities—insofar as they have the appetite for its grisly servings."

- Uche Umezurike, Author of
Double wahala, Double trouble.

"*The Strangers of Braamfontein* is a portrait of broken dreams. It is a book of piranhas destined for a fatal ending."

- Miterrand Okorie, Nigerian Abroad.

"Funny, lively and compelling characters, Onyeka Nwelue's *The Strangers of Braamfontein* is a memorable read. "

–Jumoke Verissimo, author of A Small Silence

"*The Strangers Of Braamfontein* holds up a cracked, blood-stained mirror to modern, post-colonial Africa. Tackling themes of xenophobia, homophobia, racism, sex trafficking and more, *The Strangers Of Braamfontein* lays bare the desperate lengths people will go to in search of a better life.

- Megan Thomas, Buzz Mag.

"*The Strangers of Braamfontein* is a grim, grisly view of post-Apartheid South Africa, and among its wide range of characters there are barely any who aren't morally compromised. But, for all its bleakness, it sizzles with a visceral, pulpy energy."

- Alastair Mabbott, The Herald of Scotland.

"If you want a different book, with a spotlight on a world a long way from your own back door, this is well worth a try and will linger in the memory. You can't help but keep your fingers crossed that for some, there is hope and a glimmer of light."

- Adrian Magson, The author 23
Spy and Crime Thrillers.

Onyeka's style of writing is straightforward. The *Strangers of Braamfontein* educates you, entertains you and throws harsh realities at your face. The novel portrays a typical 21st century African millennial society that exposes the tyranny of government officials and leaders. It will hook you to the end and keep you hanging on a cliff. No crime fiction comes close to this. This is simply the best I have read in a very long time.

-Chidimma Eze.

The *Strangers of Braamfontein* is a thriller. The very best of them you could possibly find out there. It is realistic and it shocks you to your roots, making you question the things you think you know. The characters are relatable. This is a strong and deeply felt novel. I

enjoyed it. I am impressed and hooked and I am sure that many others will say the same of this book.

-Daniella Eze.

The *Strangers of Braamfontein* is a well written book and the plot tells of the depth of the writer's understanding of the human condition in many African mega cities. This is a story with twists and turns that you can never predict. It keeps your heart pacing and you don't realize when you begin to take responsibility for the characters. Onyeka really gets me hooked on this one, and he has to keep this up. I can't wait for his next crime novel.

-Nwodo Henry.

Onyeka Nwelue sets a quick pace in *"The Strangers Of Braamfontein"* as he masterfully narrates the harsh realities that plays out in Braamfontein. This story is set against the backdrop of organized crime in its undiluted forms. *The Strangers of Braamfontein* is so good. It is a masterpiece and I admit that I have read it more than once.

-Chukwunyere Ejike.

I have never read anything like this written by an African. The *Strangers of Braamfontein* is a great crime tale. I will be glad if many young people read this novel. It will open their eyes to the reality of what life could possibly turn out for an immigrant in a foreign land.

-Francis Ifeanyichukwu Okwara.

No Crime Novel Comes Close To The Strangers of Braamfontein

Onyeka Nwelue knows what is at stake and he does so well with *The Strangers of Braamfontein* in portraying a 21st century Africa doomed by the sting of corruption, crime and desperation. This novel puts the spotlight on the ugly influence of intimidation, mismanagement of power by government officials and the leaders. especially their complicity in the rate at which crime and illegality attracts young people who hold onto the "get rich quick" syndrome.

Quite remarkable is the writer's figurative attempt to depict the life of drug dealing in all of its grandeur and danger, leading us on with his engaging narrative through scenes after scenes of violence, sex and betrayal.

I like his style of writing. It is straightforward. It makes you take a dive in from the first pages and excites you from the onset and all through the entire pages of the book, educating you, entertaining you and throwing harsh realities at your face. Onyeka invested well enough in vibrant characters depicting them as passionate and real. It is with this same real passion that Onyeka has written and presented this book. It

will hook you to the end and keep you hanging on a cliff. No crime fiction comes close to this. This is simply the best I have read in a very long time.

-Chidimma Eze.

This Is Onyeka's Perfect Outing As a Writer

The strangers of Braamfontein is a thriller, the very best of them you could possibly find out there. It is realistic and it shocks you to your roots, making you question the things you think you know. The action takes your breath away; you always want to know what happens next to your favourite character. It is the social and moral oddity that captures me about this book and Onyeka did a really great job in highlighting these things in ways that gets the plot going forward. Ingenious.

The characters are relatable. I mean if you have ever had an experience with the rough side of things in Africa, you will easily relate with the characters and the worlds in which they find themselves. I like it that Onyeka entertains us within surroundings that we can identify. Prostitution, drugs, human trafficking have done so much damage to societies in Africa and this is the main focus of the book. We also see it in the book that the governments of affected societies are doing nothing to stop these things. I find this to be honest and courageous of the writer and such values ought to be recognized.

The world that the writer painted in this book is a harsh one. In it, only the strongest survive. It is a jungle. A place where A world recognized for its greed, violence, betrayal, lust and ruthless use of power. Yet it is the reality that we should be strong enough to confront. It is the world of millions of people, their reality.

This is a strong and deeply felt novel. I enjoyed it. I am impressed and hooked and I am sure that many others will say the same of this book.

- Daniella Eze.

Nwelue's Breakthrough As a Writer Is This Crime Novel

The Strangers of Braamfontein is a well written book and the plot tells of the depth of the writer's understanding of the human condition in many African mega cities. His depiction of Braamfontein is no different from the realities of many others in Nairobi or Lagos or any other major African metropolitan cities where poverty is and desperation stares you in the face. Onyeka Nwelue must be a master of suspense to have achieved what he did with this book. I began reading it and it swept me off. There is hardly anything about it that isn't familiar to an observant eye. It mirrors the human condition, a testament to how easily our humanity can be eroded when we dwell for too long with hunger and desperation.

I am drawn to the character, Osas. He had left Nigeria with the hope of making it big n South Africa. But to his surprise he had exchanged one desperate level for another. Life in South Africa takes him through a story of betrayal, love, lust, and fear, all of which beams and wanes at every turn of Osas' life and with the interaction he has with every other character. Oh, and as for the other characters, they are

as indepth as Osas. I don't exactly like thinking about the Chamai character. He breaks my heart. I wish things have ended up differently for him with the closeted homosexual Chike. But instead, Chike takes advantage of his desperation and things ended up with Chamai the way it did. Really breaks my heart.

This is a story with twists and turns that you can never predict. It keeps your heart pacing and you don't realize when you begin to take responsibility for the characters. Onyeka really gets me hooked on this one, and he has to keep this up. I can't wait for his next crime novel.

- Nwodo Henry.

The Strangers of Braamfontein Is So Good

From the very beginning, Onyeka Nwelue sets a quick pace in *"The Strangers Of Braamfontein"* as he masterfully narrates the harsh realities that plays out in Braamfontein. This story is set against the backdrop of organized crime in its undiluted forms. I noticed my eyes were wet and my heart beat faster than usual as I read Ruth narrating her story to her girls, yes her girls.

I don't know why I am more drawn to the character of Ruth and her girls. Every time, there are stories of girls trafficked out of African countries by prostitution rings, sometimes unwillingly and sometimes willingly. This is one book that treats the situation in a way that entertains, questions and enlightens the reader. I am sure it should be a reference point whenever issues of trafficking and organized crime is being discussed.

I had imagined a turn of events when I got to that point where the prostitute, April, gets pregnant for Osas, the drug dealer, who also has a secret thing going with April's boss, Ruth. But then it had turned out differently and I had been left wondering how sleek Onyeka Nwelue is with spinning his plot in

such a way that made a fool of me in trying to be predictive. *The Strangers of Braamfontein* is so good. It is a masterpiece and I admit that I have read it more than once.

-*Chukwunyere Ejike.*

The Strangers of Braamfontein Is a Great Crime Tale

My favorite character is the young Nigerian, Osas, who travels to Braamfontein so as to make it big. His story is an honest depiction of the fate of millions of Nigerians and Africans who travel overseas in the hope of better lives and success. Most times they don't relate their experiences and we don't know what life for them abroad is. But with *The Strangers of Braamfontein*, we can see realities play before our eyes and we can enjoy these realities as the entertainment that they are.

I have never read anything like this written by an African. It takes a certain level of boldness to write about issues like this in such a detailed manner. Maybe this is what writing should be, and if we can look at our world as closely as Onyeka Nwelue is making us do with this book, then we can begin to have honest conversations that are channeled towards making better societies for ourselves.

The character, Papi, is another one I like. He is a clear example of what happens when we become too comfortable in predatory worlds. The jungle is what it is, and even predators could be preyed upon. I like the fact that Nwelue portrays that if ever a place have

a reputation for crime, it is so because people in high places who are supposed to protect the interests of the people who elected them there are beneficiaries of the institutionalized rot. We see this with the policemen who are on the payroll of Papi. I love what Nwelue did with this. I am impressed.

I will be glad if many young people read this novel. It will open their eyes to the reality of what life could possibly turn out for an immigrant in a foreign land.

-Francis Ifeanyichukwu Okwara.

"...Like a persistent itch that only goes away by scratching, it is hard to ignore this writer."

- Eromo Egbejule, The Guardian (UK)

"The literary world can do with more babies from the bassinet of "The Strangers of Braamfontein"!"

- Wole Soyinka, Nobel Laureate.

Praise for Burnt

"Spiders, snakes, disco, paternal violence, Jacques Brel, literary Lagos, Africans in Europe - it's a breathless series of vignettes, anecdotes and narratives we meet in OnyekaNwelue's Burnt, the whole related fast in rapidly successive moments. The voice is direct, talking you through events. Sometimes it assumes the personal, sometimes it shifts through the overheard and imagined. It is very much a multi-cultural world, the book itself a city of sorts where every window is open. So you keep watching and listening."

- George Szirtes, author of The Slant Door (1979)

"Onyeka Nwelue has written himself. These poems are vintage Onyeka: raw, honest and beautiful. Always edgy."

-Bwesigye bwa Mwesigir, author of Fables Out of Nyanja

"Daringly different and unarguably exquisite, these poems possess an unseen but felt arm that leads your entire being through boulevards decorated with brilliant narratives that keep you walking

xxiii

without stopping, but yearning for more. Here is a delectable oeuvre that resonates. One more feather on OnyekaNwelue's baronial hat. Yes."

-Echezonachukwu Nduka, author
of Echoes of Sentiments

"Sublime, strange and experimental. I read Burnt with a great admiration for Onyeka Nwelue. Each flow, each sentence, each line has something tasteless about it, yet is bewitching."

- Chika Onyenezi, author of Sea Lavender

ALSO BY THE SAME AUTHOR

1. *The Abyssinian Boy*

2. *Burnt*

3. *Hip-Hop is Only for Children*

4. *An Angel on the Piano*

5. *A Banquet for Pigs and Vultures*

6. *The Beginning of Everything Colourful*

7. *The Cuban Jazz Club*

8. *The Strangers of Braamfontein*

9. *Outside Weston Library*

10. *There Are No White People*

11. *Saving Mungo Park (with Ikenna Okeh)*

12. *The Real Owners of Britain*

13. *The Spice Bazaar*

14. *Island of Happiness*

15. *Lemon Grass*

16. *Evening Coffee with Arundhati Roy*

17. *Encounters with the Grey Maverick (with Mitterand Okorie)*

18. *A Country of Extraordinary Ghosts*

19. *The Perfect Muslims*

20. *The Nigerian Mafia: Mumbai*

21. *The Nigerian Mafia: São Paulo*

22. *The Nigerian Mafia: Johannesburg*

23. *The Fifth Night at Diggi Palace*

24. *The Last Trains Out of Ukraine*

25. *There's No Snow in Stockholm*

26. *The Peace Symphony*

27. *The Hacienda of Jesus Garcia of Pachuca.*

I dedicate this book to the great Frederick Forsyth, who inspired me and spent time in his village, sharing his experiences during the Nigeria-Biafra war

To the memory of my father, Sir Sam Nwelue

To Professor Wole Soyinka, who was jailed on his return from Biafra

To President Olusegun Obasanjo, who spent time with me, in his study, talking about the war

There is no hunting like the hunting of man, and those who have hunted armed men long enough and liked it, never care for anything else thereafter.

–ERNEST HEMINGWAY

Contents

Part III

Part IV

Part I

Part 1

*War does not
determine who is right
– only who is left.*

– BERTRAND RUSSELL

1.

The Intrusion

August 25, 1967

Ngozika's spine scraped against the concrete floor with each of the Fulani man's passionless thrusts between her thighs. She whimpered, although his palm stayed securely fastened over her mouth.

"Shut up, wench!" the soldier grunted and with a sneer. "Are you not enjoying it, wench!" His moans seemed unrealistically loud, and Ngozika could only think about her poor children tied up in the next room. They would hear his pornographic noises and the slap of his pelvis against her thighs.

Her muffled cry escaped. Despite her fingernails tearing into his wrists, she could not free herself from his weight. She tried to

bite down on his palm, but her teeth couldn't reach. Sucking in, she couldn't breathe against his grip and couldn't scream. He will smother me, Ngozika realized. He will fuck me to death, and then what will happen to my children? No matter how she squirmed, she couldn't get away. Not even her feet could force him off her.

A nocturnal bird's song pierced the terrifying darkness, undaunted by the Fulani man's grunts. She could barely hear her sobbing children in the next room. They must have gotten the tape off their mouths. Listening to her children's trauma when she was supposed to protect them was too heart-breaking. Ngozika focused on the rain pounding upon the overflowing, rusty tanks on the roof that sent a waterfall of mud-coloured water down the zinc walls and shattered window. The pummel of the water over the saturated ground was louder than the storm, but it didn't overpower the crack of the Fulani's slap across her cheek that cruelly brought her back to the present.

Tears blurred her vision, but she blinked them away. Those bloodshot eyes bore down at her—the eyes she could never forget. Ngozika had always trimmed her fingernails, but they were the only weapon she had against the soldier who overpowered her in her own home.

The whooshing winds against the ancient bungalow caused the door to rattle. Open, it swung against the wall repeatedly like an out-of-control pendulum. When the soldier had kicked it in, he likely broke the latch. How foolish she was to think that latch could ever protect her. Releasing her grip on the man's wrist, Ngozika reached with her

dominant hand to draw her fingernails across the Fulani's sweaty face.

Her howls mixed with his, and only then did he pull away. Did I miss his eyes, she worried. The soldier drew back his fist and slammed it into her cheekbone. Ngozika's vision darkened as flecks of light exploded into teeth-shattering pain. "Stop! Please, stop," she whimpered, raising her forearms to protect her face, although it didn't stop the man from beating her.

Lightning illuminated another figure as he entered through the swinging door. Oh no, is it another Nigerian solder? Ngozika's cries fell silent as dread squeezed her stomach. In her village, it was not uncommon for the Nigerian soldiers to take turns raping the women and teenage girls. Their victims often did not survive. Please, don't let that be me,

Ngozika prayed. I must protect my children. I must survive.

"Ah—! Who?" the Fulani cried, apparently as surprised by this new arrival as Ngozika was, and he tucked his erection back into his pants and scrambled for his shiny black gun. "Who goes here? Still! Stay still!"

The stranger grabbed the rapist by his uncombed Afro-style hair and yanked him across the room. Only then did Ngozika see the bloody lines across his eyes, but she couldn't stop and stare. This was her opportunity to escape.

Ngozika scrambled to stand, only to collapse before she took her first step. No! Strength, don't fail me now! There was nothing left within her. She pressed herself against the wall as the pair scuffled.

As the men grunted, the distant rumble of artillery drowned out any other sounds, leaving only the eerie silence of a war-torn landscape. Outside, a mango tree's branches brushed the zinc wall and scraped the windows, fueled by the angry gusts of the storm. A cockroach skittered across the concrete into a crevice in the peeling wall beside the Fulani's boots. Breaking apart from the stranger, the Fulani turned to run.

"Still—stay still!" the stranger commanded, but the Fulani didn't listen.

Ngozika's heartbeat thundered in her ears as a rodent ran over her foot into the cobwebby kitchen where black smoke seeped out like a dangerous secret. She'd been cooking a tuber of yam that she'd hoped to divide between her small family when the soldier kicked in the

door. Hopefully their dinner wouldn't ignite and kill them all.

The newly arrived Yoruba soldier huffed heavily, not ready for the battle to be done. Both men were around the same height, and Ngozika couldn't tell who would live. Both were dark-skinned and broad-shouldered with strength evident in their posture. Again, the pair of soldiers collided before the Fulani could reach his gun. The Yoruba kicked the black metal across the floor, out of sight.

Fiuuuuuuuuuuuuuuuuu! A bird cried, passing before the window. Or was it a leaf, blown by the angry wind? Whatever it was, a silence followed as the men wrestled. "Who…?" the Fulani grunted, gripping the Yoruba soldier's arm before he could reach the knife in his belt. "Hold on, please, can you? But who?"

13

The Yoruba soldier said nothing. Perhaps he fought for Ngozika's honor or the honour of any Biafran sister who fell under the fists of the other Nigerians. But why would he fight on behalf of the Biafrans? He slammed the Fulani into the wall, rattling the windows, but there was no bark from Power, her dog, or even any of the neighbour's dogs. In this time of starvation, maybe they'd been secretly stolen and eaten by some of the Nigerian soldiers who would not stop raping the village women.

Breaking away, the Fulani reached under the rickety chair for his gun. "Who you be?" he demanded of the newcomer. If he killed the Yoruba man, he would only come to finish what he started with Ngozika.

On wobbling legs, she tried to stand, but her knees gave out and crashed into the concrete. Not dead, she told herself. Not dead yet. But even if she could get up, would she be able to leave her children tied up in the next room to get help? Her daughter would only fall victim to the Fulani's lust if he triumphed against the Yoruba man. Even if the Yoruba man won, her daughter might fall prey to him instead. Her heart was torn.

"I said, 'Who you be?'" the Fulani asked in hurried panic, his Pidgin English full of phlegm. His back was still to the Yoruba soldier as he felt around in the dark for his gun. "Don't come at me… Don't attack, you hear?" He turned around to see the Yoruba closing in on him. "Wait. I will shoot you if you try to… dey protected, but hold on a minute, okay?"

"Shut up!" the Yoruba man snapped. He didn't have a gun, but a silver knife glinted in

the moonlight. "Freeze." His grin was made visible by a flash of lightning, his voice equally low but carried a threatening pitch. "Don't move an inch further... unless, of course, you want me to feed you with my sweets. My pockets are full of sweets, nice man. A nice man doing a nice thing to an innocent woman."

"Of course, yes!" the Fulani said with confidence, but the gun trembled in his hand.

"No, don't face me yet!" The newcomer lifted Ngozika's limp hand as if he were desiring to decipher whether she was alive or dead. Sighing, the newcomer released Ngozika's hand. "Alive, yes."

Ngozika's mind screamed at his touch. She wanted to bare her teeth, press herself against the wall, and claw his eyes out like a

frightened cat, but there was no strength left in her. She hardly mustered a groan.

"Yes, sah!" the rapist said, his voice echoing with melodramatic swiftness.

The Yoruba man ran the sharpened edge of his knife through a heart-shaped artwork on the wall, "I will waste you if you attempt to shoot. Leave the gun. Move away from the gun."

The Fulani simply stared. Was he going to obey? His arm twitched, but he didn't squat to set the gun on the concrete floor. Even when the Yoruba repeated his orders, the Fulani's arms trembled as he lifted the gun, but he wasn't fast enough. Barreling into him, the Yoruba man tackled him, knife drawn. The gun fired, sending glass raining down upon Ngozika. Her scream was a mere squeak.

Lying on his back, the rapist struggled against the newcomer. With shaking arms, the Fulani man desperately tried to keep the knife from sinking into him as the Yoruba pressed his whole weight upon it. He screamed as the knife bit into his flesh with blood spraying the wall, but he squirmed until the knife found its mark again. Finally going limp, he let his arm fall onto the floor, now reddening with his blood. The knife squelched again and again. One slice into his neck, one in his kidney, two in his chest, and two in his stomach. Blood gushed, flooding the scene of his own crime.

But someone was still crying. Ngozika's mind was slow to realize the muffled screams were coming from her two teenage children tied up in the next room. Did someone shoot Emeka and Udoka? Are my children safe? Did anybody shoot my children? No, no, no, Ngozika prayed. Christ, no.

With the rapist lying in a pool of his own blood, the Yoruba man stood, blood dripping down his blade. After watching the Fulani struggle like a decapitated fowl, the newcomer cleaned his knife on the dying man's khaki, took a deep breath, and faced Ngozika.

Has he come to save me? Ngozika prayed that he had.

The Fulani lay dead, while Ngozika lived. Did the intruder wonder if she had died too? She was not dead, but she was too weak to stand and fight, too weak to speak much. The only thing she could do was close her eyes with hopelessness and say, "Thank…"

This frailly voiced Igbo word of hers or the winds gushing into the house through the open door, snatched the words from her saliva-soaked, quivering lips and engulfed them. Again, she tried to stand, only to fall,

19

noticing for the first time the blood trickling down her leg. Although she couldn't speak, she willed the presumably sympathetic man to hurry into the living room to set Emeka and Udoka free. Perhaps the children had torn off the black tape that shut their mouths, but what about their hands, their feet, their lives? Christ, what about their lives?

Dangerous attacks like this usually brought back memories of her late husband, Nnaemeka Igbokwe, a hefty, balding, young man who had slumped on his way to their farm on her thirty-sixth birthday. This was three weeks ago, and she missed him every day since.

"I wish I had more time," the Yoruba man said, handing Ngozika the blood-smeared knife. "I have to rush off, please."

"Oh… Ah!" she groaned as he lifted her, carrying her to the battered chair the colour of decomposing groundnuts.

"Sola," he said. "My name is Sola Adenubi, a Nigerian soldier. Please use this knife to defend yourself against other Nigerian soldiers."

"Please—" she said, interrupted by gunshots in the distance. Emeka and Udoka cried weakly as the bleating of a goat accompanied their voices. Ngozika was surprised it had not been eaten yet.

Sola Adenubi glanced at her blood-stained hand. "No time, woman. Don't worry; I have a feeling you will be all right. You and your family. Bye!"

Ngozika wanted to force words out of her mouth to implore him to help her kids, to implore him to take care of her bleeding

even if it was awkward, but the soldier turned sharply like a wild animal and escaped into the night.

Crawling after him, Ngozika stumbled out the door. The moon, now breaking through the ominous clouds, hung big and beautiful above the drunkenly swaying trees. Near Ngozika's husband's grave, a Peugeot 404 rolled over dry leaves and fresh green grass. Forgetting the soldier, she rose on trembling limbs, scrambling toward the yellow, blinding torchlight. Blood dribbling down her leg, she waved both hands above her head until the car screeched to a stop.

2.

War Woes

The Peugeot 404 rattled down the road, leading the way with their yellow headlights. Even from the bus speeding behind it, the lively melody from their speakers blared in Ngozika's ears. Celestine Ukwu sang at the top of her lungs into the stillness of night.

"WOoh ooh ooh ooh WOoh ooh ooh ooh WOoh ooh ooh ooh WOoh ooh ooh ooh Onwunwa bia ọ dị ka ụwa agasia Onwunwa bia ọ dị ka ụwa ejedebe Onwunwa bia ọ dị ka ụwa agasia Onye chekwube Olisa omesia ọ g'adi mma

Onwunwa bia ọ dị ka ụwa agasia

Onwunwa bia ọ bụlụ ọlu ekwensu Onwunwa bia ọ dị ka ụwa agasia Onye welu ndidi ojesia ọ ga dị mma Añana ntị na asili ụmụ enu Añana ntị N'okwụ um'ụwa Añana ntị na asili ụmụ enu Ife imena ụmụ ụwa ga asilili Añana ntị na asili ụmụ

*enu ooh Añana nti N'okwu um'uwa Añana nti na
asili umu enu Ife imena umu uwa ga asilil..."*

The bus was rickety - a single shot from
a gun could penetrate the thin metal and kill
her, but perhaps their speed would deter the
Nigerian soldiers. Malnourished, shirtless
children and a few bearded men sang along
from the Peugeot 404 that sputtered down the
leaf-strewn, bumpy road.

*"WOoh ooh ooh ooh WOoh ooh ooh ooh
WOoh ooh ooh ooh WOoh ooh ooh ooh Onwunwa
bia o di ka uwa agasia Onwunwa bia o di ka uwa
ejedebe Onwunwa bia o di ka uwa agasia Onye
chekwube Olisa omesia o g'adi mma*

Onwunwa bia o di ka uwa agasia

*Onwunwa bia o bulu olu ekwensu Onwunwa
bia o di ka uwa agasia Onye welu ndidi ojesia o
ga di mma Añana nti na asili umu enu Añana nti
N'okwu um'uwa Añana nti na asili umu enu Ife*

imena ụmụ ụwa ga asilili Añana ntị na asili ụmụ enu ooh Añana ntị N'okwụ ụm'ụwa Añana ntị na asili ụmụ enu Ife imena ụmụ ụwa ga asilil..."

Is the driver deaf that he doesn't hear the Igbo music blaring on the speakers, Ngozika fumed inwardly, not wanting to frighten her children who sat beside her on the bus seat. Perhaps he is semi-mad. How could that moron be playing loud music—loud Igbo music—on the road in such a dangerous moment as this? He should be stopped, chained. They were only testing the Nigerian soldiers' patience.

But what choice did she have but to sit back and watch her village pass? Leaning her head back on the thin padding of the bus seat, Ngozika heaved, trying to take her mind off the drive. With three bodies crammed into a seat built for two adults, she was squeezed

close to the cracked window like a bag of rice, and she resisted grumbling her frustration.

She glanced at her wrist but found no watch. Perhaps she lost it while hurrying to board this bus with her two unabashedly weeping children who were now staring at their hands on their laps, tears long dried. They will be safe under the watchful gaze of my brother, Ngozika told herself. Chikwado knew most of her major secrets, the beautiful and the ugly, and she had not broken her promise to never air what they agreed would never be aired. He lived near her mother's home, and he would protect them.

A man turned to her from the seat in front of her family. Ngozika recognized him as the chief's older son. "Do you have any food to eat?"

Ngozika laughed. "You would take food from a widow and her children?" It wasn't as if she had anything. She'd traded a present from her husband for that yam the soldier caused her to abandon. It was the last valuable thing she owned, and it would be unlikely she would be able to get another yam easily.

Without another word, he slumped back in his seat, humming to Celestine Ukwu's song like a fool.

"I don't like Chief," Udoka mumbled, perhaps reminded by the man's son. Ngozika wondered if she had said it to herself since this was the first thing she'd said all night. The poor girl was twelve and naive to understand certain things in this world, like not speaking ill of the chief. "You didn't hear me, eh?" Udoka's voice was stronger this time after half

29

a minute of choking silence. "I really, really hate him."

This, Ngozika could not ignore, even if she wanted to. "Chief Nwafor?" She took her daughter's hand in hers.

Removing her hand in an almost disrespectful force, Udoka snapped, "Yes, Chief Nwafor." She seemed not to care if his son overheard her. "This is his name. I hate him. He touched my breast under the udara tree. Pressure, sorry. He pressed my breast and winked at me."

"He did this? It's incredible." Emeka leaned forward to watch his sister's face.

"But it happened. You are the only ones I have told, and you are the only one that will ever know. For now, at least. Please."

"Why, Udoka? Are we that special?" her brother inquired.

She looked at her folded hands atop her lap, wringing her fingers until they paled. "I hate him."

"I will see what I can do about this, but this secret will stay with me. With us. I promise you." Ngozika leaned against her in a playful manner, despite all they'd endured so far.

"Thank you."

The little family fell to silence, listening to the Igbo music making them a target to the Nigerian soldiers. Ngozika sat back in her seat, staring out the window but only seeing her memories. Why are men like that, she fumed. She's only twelve, and he's a man grown with children of his own who are older than my daughter.

But what can I do? Maybe the war will punish him, but if that's so, what have I done to deserve this?

Visions of her late husband flashed before her eyes. I wish you were here, she sighed. Her husband was never a cruel man, and certainly, he was never inappropriate toward her. Even from the first morning Ngozika had met Nnaemeka, she realized it would be difficult for them to bore one another. Together, they flew around town like overjoyed parrots, discussing the town crier, the townsmen, townswomen, discussing the laws, and the people who made them. The married men. The married women. All the people she had hated and all the people she had loved, she discussed. All the good fathers, all the good mothers. The joys of fatherhood and the joys of motherhood. The joys of being in love, of their being in love.

Ngozika had been the first to surprise the other with the gift of palm wine. He had been ridiculously excited to meet her that day as if he was an adolescent drunk with happiness. It had been both of their first excursion into romance, into love—a love that made them disobey their parents and only obey the one they loved, truly and deeply loved.

Their first date had been a journey down the stream where they both had perched on a rock to watch the fishes jump and clap the water. Ngozika and Nnaemeka had brought water pots, pretending they needed water to evade their parents' scrutiny.

The first day they went down this stream to fetch the water that they did not need, Nnaemeka held her hand the moment their feet sank into the cold, cold river and said, "Nice, nice. The features, your features. Nice, nice. How are you?"

Ngozika had smiled. She might have only been twenty, but she was used to men,

used to their words, their tricks, their schemes. She was used to shouting at annoying men, at good men, and shouting poor men away; but she did not mock Nnameka. She did not make fun of Nnameka's state of car-lessness, his lack of a bicycle or motorcycle. She had never given her jeweled hand to any man who did not have some means of transportation, let alone to accept to be his woman. "Why drink nkwu ocha when there is nkwu enu?" was her mantra. She had liked fine things and yearned to have them, calling the men who had those finer things of life Classic Men. She liked Classic Men, loved them so much with all her heart, and would have liked to marry one.

"I love you so much with all my heart," Ngozika had said, her tone fluctuating between the comic and the solemn. Sweat trickled down her cheeks, and she flicked it away with her finger. She repeated her words and searched his face.

Silence. Then Nnameka laughed, softly like the way his Igbo words moved. Softly. "I am impressed by your quick sense of humour. You love me so much, eh?"

"Of course. I can even spend the rest of my life with you." Ngozika was laughing out loud, and everyone close to her was equally laughing. A laughing, shoulder-shaking competition. How that great sense of humour and her hot temperament managed to share the same heart with such a kind man sometimes puzzled Ngozika. All the hot-tempered people she knew, and the ones she had encountered in fairytales, did not have this sense of humour. They hardly had recognized a joke when they saw one.

Just like her grandmother, just like her son Emeka, just like her friend Ijeuwa whom the water drowned and carried away. Puzzling too was her son's matchless aggression—or useless aggression—Ngozika would like to correct that behaviour with an air of dissatisfaction, but this was not the right moment for such juvenile antagonism. If only her husband still lived, he was a good man and would have been a good example for her son to look to instead of the soldiers who were all around.

Ngozika wanted to ask Emeka how he was caught by the stabbed Nigerian soldier, the rapist, and how he succeeded in tying him and her sister up. But she did not ask her son this question.

I wish Nnaemeka could be here now. Ngozika's throat tightened with a threat of a

sob. He was a kind man, a soft man, and she wished she could beg the man to come back to life to be with her, fight with her, and cry with her. She would like to tell him that his son, her son, Emeka, the stubborn tiger-looking Emeka was a cold-blooded animal that had sworn to defile the law of change. Nnaemeka would then lean on her shoulder to ask her why the boy would dare disobey her. How dare the boy walk out of the house while she was still shouting? How dare the boy go into the bushes to hunt without informing her? How dare the boy sell the meat and share the rest without bringing a chunk home? How dare the boy throw a stone at a limping elderly woman who reprimanded him for not greeting her?

But Ngozika did not disinherit him, and she never would. "Love is magic. Love forgives. Love endures," her husband had said

on the day they met, or the year they met, she could not remember. She only recalled the sun shining on his sweaty face like a work of art when he spoke those words. He'd been like a shy little girl with a flower in her hair, avoiding her unblinking eyes, yet speaking coherently and fluently as though his line had been thoroughly rehearsed.

"He copies your traits," Chikwado, her brother, had said of Emeka one moonlit evening beneath a guava tree outside their mother's home. The air had reeked of goat dung, but the winds had come with dew, leaving them shivering.

Ngozika had sneezed, and he had smiled, lit by moonlight. Wiping her nose with her finger, she had snapped, "Which means I am a bad woman?"

"We both know it was a joke," he had said, laughing nervously. The moth circling the oil lamp in the darkened compound dropped to the brownish soil and curled like a burnt piece of paper.

"It better be a joke," she said with faux joviality, and a leaf left the tree and drifted into his elephant tusk filled with palm wine. "Emeka is fiercer than a tiger."

Chikwado nodded with mournful clumsiness and lifted his tusk to his lips.

"He loves me so much, but I almost killed him with a violently flung kitchen knife."

"Nnaemeka?" Chikwado laughed, seeming shocked.

"It happened two months after my traditional marriage to Nnaemeka. He was correcting me in a raised voice. I was wrong because I ate his food, spent his budget, and

laughed endlessly with the handsome man who won the New Yam Festival's Wrestler of the Year Award while he shivered in the bedroom. But he didn't hit me. What he did was scream when my knife ricocheted off the door behind him. I asked him to stop talking, but he continued, so I threw the knife. I was angry. Furious. It's my greatest weakness, my only depressing weakness. I wish I could defeat anger. I am afraid I might anger him one day, and he would raise his voice, and I will throw a knife and something dangerous like that."

Chikwado had heaved and scratched his sweaty forehead. "Your chi will always pour water on your flaming temperament."

This, of course, had happened when Ngozika's husband was alive. Now he was dead, and she sat within the shaky bus on

the way to Ogwuma behind the car with the blazing radio. She liked that almost all the people on the bus prayed that God would roast all the Nigerian soldiers that shot at innocent Igbo children. She prayed that her children, all her children, would live to tell their story, this story. But when she opened her eyes, their tear-stained cheeks reminded her of the trouble they'd endured.

She wished she could have her children all to herself so that if a bomb was detonated on the vehicle, she would go up as ashes with her children, not with this crayfish-smelling chief's son sitting in the seat in front of her. He was narrating to the woman sitting across from him how his heart broke as the bombed buildings collapsed on his friend Joe and crushed him into the soil.

But Ngozika wished the man could stop so that everybody would have a chance to try to hear her heart crumble as the rain continued to water her husband's grave. She was not known for this, for this sentimentality, but here she was.

This bus, when it galloped again, brought to mind the last scene in Ernest Hemingway's novel, *The Sun Also Rises*. The book might not have been her favourite novel, but Ernest Hemingway was by far her favorite. *The Sun Also Rises* happened to be the book she was reading when the Nigerian-Biafran war began, and now she, like the protagonist in the novel, Jake, was in a vehicle.

If the couple behind her were inclined to literature, Western literature, she would say, "Isn't it pretty to think so?" to bring an air of elite cheerfulness into this suffocating vehicle

42

and see if they could forget their plight, but the man and his wife were clearly illiterate like most Biafrans and Nigerians. She closed her eyes, and that memorable question ("Isn't it pretty to think so?") echoed against the walls of her mind. It interested her that the speaker, Jake, referred to the idea that he and Brett, the object of his attraction, could have had "a damned good time together."

She had felt sorry for Jake when she had closed the book, and now, to her surprise in this situation of hopelessness, her heart went to the author. What could have pushed the great man of letters to take his own life? She wished she could take her own life, but who would care for her kids? Who would give them the education they craved? She had no formal education, but she could read big books, including encyclopaedias and dictionaries. Virtually all the women she knew could not read or write. Her gratitude would always go to her grandfather who taught her in her childhood. The old man did not fly overseas, but he had worked with the Pink people in Onitsha and in Lagos. It was a publishing company that printed newspapers and magazines. But the old man had transitioned, his son had transitioned, and she, the wife, would soon transition if this war continued.

Her son, sitting on the other side of his sister, seemed to read her thoughts, her dark thoughts. "Stop thinking about death."

"Oh God," she said and tore off some strands of hair. They fell off her hands like odd black petals.

Staring out the window, Ngozika squinted into the rainy darkness until her worst fears became visible in the distance. The driver stepped on the brake with ominous suddenness, and the men on the bus asked him, in panicky tones, to reverse and take the road by his left side. With squealing tyres, the bus turned, rumbling off-road, crushing tins and bottles and singing praises for God. The melodious voice of Celestine Ukwu had retreated, and the air reeked of soured foods and rotten things.

When they appeared on the tarred road, she glanced to the side to see if her children were dozing. Udoka held Emeka, and the boy, as always, was looking out the window with an expression of stoic heroism.

"The fire burnt the barn?" Emeka asked to split the clumsy silence that sat around them like tattered things.

"Everything!" Ngozika recalled with a start the black smoke coming from her kitchen. Hopefully, the fire would run out

of fuel and sputter to die. Glancing out the window, Ngozika leaned forward in her seat. The sky was grey in parts but mostly creamy and whitish, like smoke. Black birds circled the sky, and some dived into the green grasses and the dust-coated trees flying by as the car galloped.

"Everything?" Emeka asked.

Ngozika sighed, then searched her son's face. He was so thin and tall, but she was not tall. She had the body of a woman who fed four times a day, even though she could not remember the last time she ate twice. Her gown, lemon and torn, was what she wore the day her husband died. He had bought it for her, which made it even more special. But she was not interested in romantic sentimentality now. She would have liked to change her clothing and her children's, which were worse. Theirs were black rags, and their faces, like their hands, were shriveled as if they belonged to old people. But theirs were not the worst; many children of Biafra already had swollen bellies, and hopefully Emeka and Udoka would be saved in her village.

Ngozika glanced at her son who was staring at her with curiosity and said, "You heard me right. Everything."

"You sound like you're angry with me," he said, ignoring the prying eyes of other passengers. "I am not the Nigerian soldiers that set it on fire, am I? Why are you angry with me?"

Black smoke seeped into the bus through the broken windows, and she waited for the winds to blow them away before she said, "I am angry with everything God created. Everything."

"It's all right, Mama," he said, coughing with a few people on the bus. "It's all right."

The journey became less depressing when a black-coated and white-haired man rose from the first row of seats and asked everybody to close their eyes for prayers. "We need to hand this journey into the capable hands of our Lord Jesus Christ," he said and coughed. "Many of us are corpses down there. I mean, from where we came. Many of us are corpses, but we are alive on this bus, running away from danger and to safety. God is with us. God is still with us. Let us pray for consistent grace and worship his infinite kindness and grace. Amen?"

"Amen!" the passengers chorused, and Ngozika looked round to see their faces. Most of these Christians, Ngozika observed, were women: young women, married women, bandaged women, pregnant women, and women with little children. Very few men responded. But she was not in the mood to ponder or speculate the reason or reasons why broken women, these broken women, were keener on God than men, these equally broken men.

Ngozika imagined her husband decomposing in the grave near his house, and a cold thing sank in her heart. She closed her eyes and visualized him sitting next to her on the bus.

Nnaemeka? she asked in a delighted tone, a stone rolling off her heart. Nnaemeka?

He put his hand on her shoulder and said, in English: Yes, darling. It is me. And I have missed you.

You have changed. Your beard, your eyes, your skin.

49

What happened to them? he asked, rubbing his unkempt beard and staring at his shrivelled hands.

God, you have changed. Nobody was feeding you? Are you hungry?

Her husband laughed, a short ghostly laugh. Then he said: We don't eat food over there.

Our children cry every day. They miss you. They need you. Look. See them, Emeka and Udoka.

I will be with them when their own time comes. This is your moment.

Ngozika leaned into him to cuddle, but something—what was it?—restrained her. She said: When will you come back to stay with us? To stay with us forever?

Until you learn to control your anger, he joked.

But she did not laugh. She only mumbled: Okay. Okay.

I am sorry if my joke was insensitive, he said, running his hand through her hastily combed hair. Where are you going to? Where is the bus going to?

I am going to my village with our children, she answered.

Until the war is over? he asked.

She moved closer to him to see if he wore his favorite Tony Montana perfume, and he did. She usually sniffed him when they were close like this and he smelled nice, but now she only frowned and said: The war will never be over.

Don't be angry, he said. And don't be pessimistic, you hear? Do not be pessimistic.

The war will never be over, she said. We are all going to die. The world will burn to ashes. That is what the Nigerian soldiers want, right? The world can destroy itself for all I care.

Our children are in this world. And you, my love, are also in this world.

I can go to hell. Everybody can all go to hell. Ngozika crossed her arms.

Her husband shook his head, then said: Take it easy on yourself, Ngoo. I wish I had some money. You look hungry. You need to eat. It hurts…it hurts me that there is no food again.

Gunshots echoed in the distance, and Ngozika whipped her head to the window. When she turned back to Nnaemeka, he was gone, replaced by her terrified children. Everyone on the bus, including the two muscular men standing tall and bold near the entrance with guns, screamed, and their frightened voices brought Ngozika back to the world of reality.

"Slow down, driver!" Ngozika shouted.

The driver, a pot-bellied old man with a balding head and a toothpick in his mouth, turned with a look of murderous rage and returned his gaze to the road. Gunshots crackled behind them, then there was an explosive burst that rattled the already broken windows. Ngozika knelt on the seat, looking out the back window as a building collapsed into a cloud of smoke and debris.

The screams rose again, but the passengers didn't care to witness the building's dying gasp as it was reduced to rubble. Although some

men and women pleaded with the driver to be allowed to jump off through the window and run to safety, he said nothing. The bus continued to rumble down the dusty road on the way to Ogwuma.

Ngozika's eyes burned with tears that never came. *Nnaemeka was too good for this world, and now he waits for me in death. This war will never end,* Ngozika blinked rapidly to keep the tears from filling her eyes. If Nnaemeka had been home when the Nigerians had come, he would have been killed when he tried to protect her. Without a gun or knife, he would have been overpowered, and she would be alone again.

This war will never end, she sighed.

3.

Dickens of Death

Gunshots crackled in the distance. Is nowhere safe? Ngozika sniffled as a tear dripped down her cheek.

Sitting on a turquoise sculpture in front of the house Ngozika's father had built before he joined his ancestors, Ngozika massaged her swollen ankle. Although the home was a mud square surrounded by palm trees, it was spacious and decorated with cowries and peacock feathers. A custodian of art, her father had been called in his time. The wooden door was a celebration of primary colours and cowries. The only inelegant object used in building the house was the thatch that had caught fire one Harmattan that was saved thanks to Ngozika who had seen it in time and ran to fetch a bucket of water.

Ngozika turned in time to see her son step out of the doorway, blinking rapidly in the sunlight. He walked toward her, eating a roast corn. "I am sorry you are hurt, Mum," Emeka said, his voice uncharacteristically soft and tender. A butterfly, white and purple, dipped up and down close to his face, and he caught it with an aggressive hand, crushed it, and dropped it. He stepped on it and spat, but the saliva did not land on the dead butterfly but a yellowing leaf that had dropped from the mango tree nearby.

Gunshots startled Ngozika and her son, but they did not run. Where else could they go? There was nowhere else. This was the safest spot she could think of.

She wiped her tears on the sleeve of her torn mauve gown and asked, "Where is Udoka?"

"She is hiding in the room with Grandma," Emeka said and spat again. Another butterfly fluttered past, but he could not catch it. It flew up when he attempted to crush it in his hands and vanished into the sky which had turned grey with smoke.

"What about Chikwado?" she asked and blinked until tears dropped onto her lap and trickled down her thigh. Emeka looked away. But she did not cover herself properly. She would not cover herself properly. She was not in the mood for decency. What she needed was peace—or to be honest, death. But who would take care of Udoka and Emeka? Who would have the courage to dig another grave in her late husband's house to bury another human being? Wasn't it last month when her husband was lowered into his grave? She coughed and wiped her tears with her dirty palm.

Emeka coughed and slapped the cloud of smoke coming his way. "Uncle Chikwado is roasting a lizard at the backyard. He says he can eat it. How can a human being eat that thing?"

"He asked you to eat one?"

Emeka frowned, and his eyes narrowed. "He is my uncle, but if he told me to eat a lizard, I would slap him."

Shut up Ngozika thought but said, "Control your tongue."

A pregnant woman with a baby tied to her back hurried past the compound, her hands on her head in despair, and she wailed, "My husband! My husband!"

Ngozika did not know who the woman was, but she suspected it was the married woman whose husband kicked her back to her father's house because she was "lazy and lousy" but later brought back home after listening to the advice of the elders. Only God knows how long she cried, Ngozika thought. Only God knows what has happened to her husband and why she is crying. Only God knows if she hasn't gone mad.

An ear-splitting gunshot was fired, and the pregnant woman screamed and turned to run back. Someone groaned indoors, and Ngozika looked back to see if it was her mother, but she couldn't see beyond the grey smoke curling over the thatched roof.

Emeka coughed, a fake cough this time, and rose. "Amaka. Her name is Amaka. She is Mazi Okeke's wife. Maybe the man has died. A lot of men are dying. But women are not dying."

Ngozika brought her bowl from under her seat. "But women are not dying?"

61

"You are still crying, Mum?"

"But women are not dying, Emeka?"

"Do you think I am praying so that you will die? Ah, Mummy!"

She studied the boy's face and said with puerile annoyance, "I also noticed that women are not dying. Only men. Sons are not dying."

"We are dying, Mum," Emeka said with an emotive stare. "Look at me. Am I alive?"

The words were fast and sharp; jolting the crevices of her heart. "I am sorry…"

"It is okay, Mummy. Mama wants… "

"I don't want anything," Mama Ngozika said, approaching.

Ngozika shook her head but held her tongue. Her mother was the most garrulous and boring human being she had ever seen, but regardless, she still loved her. The war was going on, but she could not stop talking about chickens that fell into stagnant water and drowned. She believed that the war was fake, and God would protect His people. She would cite the Scripture and pontificate about the God of Samuel, Joshua, and David. There was no conversation she would meet and fail to find her way into it with her ignorant and often preposterous opinions. But she had a sense of humour, which Ngozika admittedly lacked.

The old woman was light-skinned and wrinkled, but her eyes were still full of youthful excitement and mischief. She had not been eating well like most people in the village, but Ngozika did not think one could easily see that. Perhaps it was because the old woman was already all bones and had begun to limp. The wrapper she wore was the colour of sunlight, but there were red dots all over

it. Blood? Oil? Ngozika did not know and did not bother to ask. Her ankle, just like her vagina, still hurt. She could not remember where she hit her leg while struggling with the Nigerian soldier that raped her. When her mother asked her, she said she did not know, but her daughter said, "Mum? I think you hit it at the centre table. There are bad nails all over that ugly furniture."

What is Udoka doing by the way? Ngozika thought, but before she could ask the question, Emeka blurted, "But, Grandma, you told me that you want something."

"What? What? " Mama Ngozika asked, blinking.

"Faith," Emeka said and removed the dead fly from the old woman's white hair. "You said that you want faith to be planted in us."

"I was only joking," the old woman said with a laugh, and Ngozika saw that her teeth had become yellower. Perhaps her mother had been eating some hidden food? No, no, she was not like that. She would rather starve than watch her daughter and grandchildren starve. But what coloured her yellow teeth? Palm oil? What palm oil? Whose palm oil? Everything, including water, seemed scarce in this time of war.

"How is your leg, Ngoo?" her mother asked.

Ngozika rubbed her ankle and looked up. "Good, Mama. It's good. I am good. Good inside."

"Don't push me away," the old woman said, frowning.

"I am not pushing you away," Ngozika said.

"Your words are pushing me away, but I am stubborn."

Emeka chuckled. "Stubborn."

The old woman turned to Emeka with a grin. "Very stubborn. I am very stubborn. I will not run away from my village because of this so-called war. It is fake, believe me. The Bible says that God cannot allow what is bigger than you to happen to you. Wars are bigger than us, see? God can God-fold His hands and watch us poor Igbo people suffer? Impossible."

"Go inside, Mama," Chikwado walked from the back of the house and said. He picked his teeth with a fingernail, and he stopped beside Emeka.

"Okay, okay," the old woman said and limped into the house. The door shut and seconds later, her transistor radio began to blare:

The war is here! The Nigerian soldiers have entered Onitsha. Entered Owerri. Entered Nsukka. The war is here, and every Biafran should dig something, a bunker, and prepare for it. Ojukwu has a solution, but we must act fast and wisely. Dig and hide, oh Igbo people!

"I can dig," Emeka said and bent to take his mother's shaking hands. "I can dig, Mummy."

"I can dig too." Chikwado forced a smile for Ngozika's sake, but would it be safe here? She'd brought her children here to be safe, but gunshots shattered the stillness.

"I see," she said in English and returned to her injury. The boy stood, watching her, and saying nothing. And she wondered what went on in his mind. Perhaps the lad thought she was ignoring him and waiting for death (which seemed imminent), but he could not,

at his age, understand that looking at one's once-handsome child and seeing the bones within the shriveled body was excruciating.

The boy was shirtless and filthy; his shorts were tattered and soiled. Flies buzzed musically around his bare feet as though he had accidentally stepped into faeces. Ngozika's nostrils were full of mucus, but she could perceive the unpleasantness which had mingled with the odour of burning things. The rotten cobs of corn were burning behind the building. The fallen thatch covering for their goats (which had already been slaughtered and eaten) also burned in the fire. Perhaps Emeka had thrown other things into the fire or roasted something there.

Some Igbo people had begun to hunt for lizards and other animals they had never eaten before the war, only leaving the fish and snakes which were revered. The smoke, now grey and thick like clouds, had filled the air, and Ngozika tried unsuccessfully not to cough. She did not want to cough because she was frail, exhausted, and famished. The only food in the house—nsala soup with no fish— went to her children and their grandmother. She managed two almost rotten pears and a cob of maize. She had lost weight, she knew, and she would continue to lose weight like her children.

Now she looked surreptitiously at Emeka, then lowered her head. Her tears dropped on the sandy soil. Emeka, this boy standing before her and chewing his corn, could not be her son. God, he could not be her son. These were her thoughts, but of course, the boy was hers. She could see his ribs and some of the greenish veins and thick bones in his chest and neck.

"Ichie Okorie died this evening," Emeka said.

Ngozika looked up, her eyes blurry with tears. "Jesus Christ."

It was intended to be an exclamation, but she was too weak to raise her voice. Emeka squatted and said, "He died so that the food would be enough for his children. Udoka told me. She said that Grandma told her this. And I believe them. Why didn't they tell you? I asked them why they didn't tell you, but they…"

"I know, I know," she said, interrupting the boy. "Ichie Okorie is lucky wherever he is. Death is better than being alive."

"Mama?"

"What?"

"You are crying, Mama."

70

The words he used hurt her. She had thought that the boy had seen the tears in her eyes. Why wasn't he paying attention? Why was this boy a cold-blooded animal? He might sound compassionate, Ngozika thought, but deep down, he was not. Perhaps he was trying to appear amiable, living and caring so that he would always have the most food. But what food? Where would they find food? Everyone was starving and dying.

The word "dying," unfortunately reminded her that Ichie Okorie had passed. This was an upright man. A man who stopped and fought some terrible youths who wanted to rob her grandma. He had caught them sneaking into her home one night and ran in with a cutlass. He did not slaughter any of them, but some lost their ears and fingers.

71

Ichie Okorie was one of the few literate folks in the village. His favourite novelist was Charles Dickens ("I named my first son Pip, after Philip or Pip in *Great Expectations*, though I shouldn't be giving my child a white man's name!") and nicknamed his wife Oliver Twist. This was because the woman was unfaithful to him; she was cheating on him with the best hunter in the village, the best palm wine tapper in the neighbouring village, the best farmer in the clan, and the best wrestler she had ever seen. She had died during childbirth, but he did not remarry.

Several people thought that he would have an affair with Ngozika because his wife was adulterous, but Ichie Okorie was the last man to cross the sacred boundary and into such an abomination. He and Ngozika only met to discuss literary characters. He used to mock her because she preferred a writer who took his own life, but didn't Ichie Okorie take his own life? How ironic.

Or did he die a natural death? No, Ngozika could not believe this. Ichie Okorie, her husband, and many others had left her in this world that was constantly shaken by the blasts of bombs and gunshots. There were still gunshots in the distance, but her legs could not run. And she supposed it was the same problem of fatigue that held her daughter, her son, and her mother. But even if she could run, where would she escape to? It was better for the Nigerian soldiers to kill them in their house than do it on the road or in the bushes. She would not dash off again and stumble into another bus.

When the frightening sounds of gunshots had subsided, Emeka said, "Let me go and dig at the backyard, Mum."

Chikwado put a hand on her shoulder to guide her. "Go inside! Hide!"

Ngozika abandoned her bowl and towel, and she did as her mother did and limped inside. The gunshots continued.

4.

Singing Sadness

The Chief Priestess of Oguta Lake Goddess, Ogbuide, was surprised but delighted to be consulted by someone in this dangerous time when people were dying like flies. Perhaps she was not that happy to meet a new admirer, Mama Idu thought. She believed that native doctors, priestesses, and foreseers relished the visits and consultations of people from far and near places and villages. Those consultations beckoned the potency of one's spiritual powers and trust. Yes, the goddess of Oguta, Ogbuide was a powerful woman, a harmless woman, but Mama Idu's heart thumped the moment she stepped into the chief priestess' house.

Mama Idu had prepared for this consultation with the chief priestess, but now her heart hung with a desperate thumping her chest.

The walls in the chief priestess' house were beautiful with palm leaves and festooned with both white and red cloths. The lovely décor warmed Mama Idu's heart. Beautiful, too, were the cowries tied around her sticks and palm leaves. The chief goddess herself relaxed on what looked to be a goatskin mat.

Mama Idu saw that her friend Ngozika was right when she said that the chief priestess was almost always donned in white. Today, the priestess wore a white scarf—or was that really a scarf? Small like a precious stone and still undiscovered by people. But wrinkles had begun a very depressing attack on the goddess' shiningly gorgeous ebony skin. They were prominent on her face, these pimples, but one could see that she was an astonishing picture in the days of her youth. Her beaded anklet glistened in the sunlight, but the beads she sewed into her shiny white skirt did not.

Mama Idu moistened her lips to speak, but words failed her. The sun, streaming in through an open window, was behind her like an overripe orange, and in Mama Idu's eyes. Goats bleated somewhere, fowls squawked, and the unpleasant odour of animal dung was thick in the air. The gunshots that followed Mama Idu had ceased, but some still reverberated in her eardrums.

Her friend, Ngozika, had called her a coward, and secretly Mama Idu agreed. Miraculously, she had learned to live with the gunshots since the war had begun. But the dead bodies of the children and some adults flung across the dusty and serene road of Oguta, which she had used with trepidation,

and the flies that circled them would haunt her until she left this world to join her ancestors.

"The great goddess of the water," Mama Idu said, in Igbo, and prostrated as Ngozika had seriously advised. *Nzu* dropped from her pocket, but she ignored it. She could not remember putting it into her breast pocket, but she had played with it in her grandfather's *obi*.

"You are welcome, my daughter," Ogbuide said and studied Mama Idu's *nzu* with unblinking eyes. "This is Priestess Ogbuide, as I imagine you know, my daughter. Who are you, please? You look familiar."

"Familiar? I look familiar?"

The chief priestess plucked something—a bitter kola, perhaps—and began to chew it. "Very familiar."

"My friend Ngozika directed me to your house," Mama Idu said and scratched her head with a trembling finger. "She is that aggressive woman who lost her husband a few weeks ago."

"Oh, sit down first," Priestess Ogbuide said with surprising promptness, gesturing to a black couch littered with red candles and chicken feathers. "Sit down, please. Shift those things—the candles, and—yes, yes. And then sit. Sit down."

Mama Idu turned up her nose at the faint smell of blood and kola nuts in the house. Two teenagers, a tall but thin boy and his short and fat sister, stood at the door, their eyes fixed on their mother and not Mama Idu. She had not been informed the adolescents were the children of the priestess, but the striking similarities of their almost European noses,

ebony skins, and oval faces were instantly reassuring.

Soon their mother called them (Ikenna and Ada) and asked them to help her get the bottled hot drink atop the tall white fridge pushed against the wall. They brought the bottle, two very small glasses, and two sachets of cold water from inside the fridge. When they left, they discussed a popular wrestler who had fallen from a mango tree and broken his legs, and Mama Idu imagined the siblings climbing trees to get some fruits for him.

Hunger made her stomach grumble every now and again, but she was not here for food. After the visitor had been served the alcohol, after a proper but brief introduction and commentaries on the ongoing war and hunger, after sipping the hot drink and ah-ing, the goddess cleared her throat and said, "We

know that a toad does not run in the daytime for nothing…"

"Yes, of course," with a forced smile, Mama Idu interrupted.

The chief priestess lowered her head, then lifted it with a dramatic flourish. "Good, good."

"I thank you for this warm welcome," Mama Idu said with sincerity.

The goddess fanned herself. "Warm welcome? Thanks, but you sound like you want to leave."

"No, no. I have just arrived."

"Oh, you are a joker!"

They both laughed, and Mama Idu thought: Thank God she likes my subtle sense of humour and confidence.

But Mama Idu's voice had a trace of tremor when she said, "The goddess, for days... two days, I think. Two and a half. My only child—my only son—is missing. He is only ten years old and deaf. He told me he was going to the stream to fetch water and hunt for birds, but I have not seen him since. I've been apprehensive since his disappearance. What should I do? How can we discover where he is? And whether he is still alive or dead? Or dead, God!"

"Your child is still alive," Ogbuide said with confidence. "He will return home before the next market day, believe me. But you'll know what I mean soon. A few days after this visit."

Mama Idu said, "How did you know...? Sorry, I meant how can I know? I meant how

84

can I be convinced—confident that my boy Mark is still alive?"

"You will remember my words in the end," Ogbuide said, after staring at the ceiling for a moment. "What is his Igbo name?"

Mama Idu dodged the buzzing bee coming at her face and said, "Uche. Uche is his Igbo name, but we always call him Mark."

"Uche… Uche… Uche. A young boy with a lot of potential. Be strong. You will find the boy."

Mama Idu wondered if the goddess and her friend Ngozika were somehow related. Same confidence, same poise, same intimidating physique. Be strong. This was Ngozika's favourite phrase. Be strong; your broken water pot can be forgiven. Be strong; your father will stop beating your mother. Be

strong; your feverish condition will fade away. Be strong here and there. Consistently.

"Thank you," Mama Idu said and lowered her glass to the cement floor.

The priestess called the two children to come and return their glasses to the fridge. But it took them almost one minute to appear and do what they were asked to do. After they had returned to their bedroom, Mama Idu asked the goddess, "I pray that your son will not be conscripted into the army. Such a handsome boy. Just like my Mark."

The priestess grinned, and Mama Idu, for the first time, saw the gap in her teeth. "If they want him to fight for our land, let him fight. Isn't he a boy? Nothing will happen to him. He will go to the battlefield and come back alive."

"Amen."

"Faith is very important in life."

"Are you sure I will find my son?" she asked, leaning back on the couch hopelessly.

"Em, what's your name again?" Priestess Ogbuide asked with undisguised annoyance.

And Mama Idu straightened at once. "I am sorry, but… but I worry that the Nigerian soldiers… Maybe they have killed him. They are killing us, mothers, fathers, and even children. I saw many dead bodies on my way to your house. And we can hear gunshots. Listen." She craned her neck.

"The Nigerian soldiers can never capture Oguta," Ogbuide said with characteristic confidence.

"Really?"

"They will drown if they ever try to."

"Oh."

"Yes. I am serious. The Nigerian soldiers will get drowned if they try to capture Oguta. You speak like a stranger."

Mama Idu heaved. "Thank you, Priestess. I owe you a lot. I don't even know what to offer you."

The Chief Priestess got up. "I will do something for you. Come again after the next market day."

"Okay. Thanks."

When Mama Idu stepped out of the house, it was raining softly. Hopefully, Mama Idu prayed, the water from the sky will drown the bloody Nigerian soldiers and carry their corpses back to their regions.

At home, she went straight to the bathroom to bathe. The bathroom—if one could call it one—was a little bigger than a big cupboard, and the walls were made with rusty zinc. The floor was made of cement but was perilously slippery. Her husband had slipped in this bathroom, hit his head on the floor, and died. But she still went in here to bathe. Was this courage? Her friend Ngozika had asked her to demolish it, but who would do that for her? There was no money in the house, and things had gotten worse since the beginning of the war. She bent towards the iron bucket, scooped some water, and poured the cold thing on her body. Shivering, she sang a song she had composed in her head the previous day.

"I have no child in this world,

I have no husband in this world,

I have no life and no joy,

But I have you, my God.

My friend Ngozika may disappoint me tomorrow,

But you will never do that.

Kindly give me the strength to carry on,

Kindly give me the grace to move through life like water,

Kindly reset my brain so that I can forget all that has happened to me…"

She continued singing until she was done bathing, then carried her bucket and walked out of the bathroom with extreme care. But in the bedroom, she resumed her singing, this time with tears in her eyes and in her voice. The geckoes on the peeling, unpainted walls hurried into the dilapidated ceilings and hid. There was nothing in the bedroom except her spring bed, a basket of clothes, and a sewing machine her husband had bought for her on her birthday two years ago. The bedroom still smelt of him, and that hurt.

90

He had bought the sewing machine for her because he thought that sewing was lucrative. He had never believed in her talent, which was singing. She needed a piano, but he bought a sewing machine. Never even a hoe, for they were farmers, but a sewing machine. Perhaps one of his friends had a wife who was great at sewing, and he envied that. Or perhaps he had a secret mistress who was a seamstress? No, no, no, she thought. Papa Idu cannot have cheated on me. He was not like Ngozika's late husband. The man had once tried to proposition her, but she slapped off his hand. She did not tell her friend about this, and she would never tell her. It might destroy their friendship, she believed, and that friendship was the most important thing she had on earth right now.

She sang her song again, and after singing, she modified the lyrics. "Ngozika" was replaced with a fictitious name: "Aisha." Then she wore her blue skirt and white polo and climbed into bed.

5.

Running Beserk

Sitting on her bed in the long-abandoned house that had belonged to Ngozika's late husband, she covered her mouth and nose with the cloth of her dress. Already, the dead body of her rapist reeked, its smell permeating into every room. Ngozika clenched her jaw to keep from gagging.

When she had arrived at sunset from her mother's house, nobody was outside, and to her relief, nobody was inside her home either. The entire compound was as silent as a graveyard. Perhaps it had become a graveyard after the death of this Fulani bastard, Ngozika thought, retreating to the doorway with only the slightest trepidation. Perhaps the bastard's evil spirit has attracted the ghosts of other dead rapists.

The door, as she pushed it, creaked and fell off with a cloud of decay, dust, and smoke. Do I dare look, she thought. She had seen a dead body when her husband left this world and others in her time, but none that had violated her and died in front of her. Unclamping her eyes, she allowed her gaze to land on the lump of putrid flesh on the concrete floor of her living room. The last rays of the setting sun illuminated the body of the Fulani soldier.

Ngozika spat and cursed to be reminded of that night. Had she truly forgotten? And why did she forget about it, about an unforgettable traumatizing event in her life? Oh, the war, she would like to say. Oh, the war. The war was the cause of everything. She crossed over the body to the broken door swinging on its hinge and walked across the dead leaves to a guava tree. Before sitting on a dust-coated bench, she cleaned the furniture with her handkerchief. Who will help me get rid of that dead body? she thought as she looked around. Who will fling this body into the other rubbish where it can never be seen by a human eye?

The dry leaves scattered about the compound scratched the hardened mud as the winds moved with whistling sounds. Emeka is bold, she thought, but could Emeka bundle the corpse for her and throw it out of sight and where its foul smell would be abandoned? The sun would go down completely soon. But the only lamp in the house had been stolen or misplaced. She would have to return to her father's house or suffer the disgusting horror of sleeping in the same house with a corpse, a ghost, and blood.

If not that her mother was childish and infuriating, she wouldn't have come back to her late husband's house to spend a few days or weeks. Any moment that could take her mind off the pranks and rants of her mother. The old witch had come into her bedroom one blustery night and screamed, "Hide, young Biafrans! The Nigerian soldiers are coming with ammunition and the bleeding heads of our people!"

The first person to run out of the house shrieking had been Ngozika. The second had been the old woman, then the boy, then the girl. Her children. The old woman was laughing. The boy and the girl panted, but Ngozika fell to her knees like a woman gunned down at the waterfront. The old woman stopped laughing when Ngozika began to shout in fluent Igbo:

98

"So you wanted to kill me with your shameless, puerile prank? You think you are a teenager or what? It's about time you stopped acting a clown and throwing your stupid pranks at us! What's wrong with you, Mama? Have you gone mad? I am asking you! Have you gone mad!"

"Mama, honestly, this is stupid!" Emeka said, his eyes full of blood-painted arrows. "What if we harmed you? I wish I could flog you. I wish I could break something on your head…"

"Enough!" Udoka shouted at her brother before bursting into tears.

"Now, Ngozika my daughter, I agree with your opinion that I am old, and like other old people, I have begun to return to my childhood," the old woman said with pretentious modesty and faux pathos. "I am

acting like a child. Yes, adulthood is childhood. You were right. You are right. Mama Ngozika is a baby. A baby in a lap, sucking Mummy's breasts."

Ngozika staggered towards her mother. "All these jokes of yours are stale and ludicrous! This is not the time to be silly!"

"Mummy, stop!" Udoka implored her mother. "I don't like how everybody is shouting at Mama."

The old woman brushed off Ngozika's hand and turned searchingly for her granddaughter. "Oh, dear Udoka! You have the heart of a dove. Kind and innocent. I love you, my dearest. You are not like your mother. You resemble me. You are the only human being in this house who supports my ambition to be a comedian. Your mother is

envious. It's obvious that they are envious. Everybody knows—"

Wall-shaking gunshots flashed to the sky and tore the silence into pieces. The pieces had not fallen to the ground, but everybody except Emeka had hurried into the house screaming the name of Jesus. Ngozika, thinking about the incident now, wondered why Emeka refused to rush indoors and out from the bullets. Maybe the lion was prepared to face the entire kingdom and defeat them or die once and for all to quit this excruciating reality in which he tiptoed like a rain-drenched rodent on a path littered with sharp pins. But soon the boy, the drowning boy they only knew as Emeka, entered the living room with a gun.

"Lock the door!" Ngozika whispered in a continued panic. "Bolt it… and don't talk!"

The boy obeyed, but his sister said, shivering at the door leading to the bedroom, "This gun again, Emeka? Okay, lock the door first."

"Whose gun?" Ngozika asked, approaching the boy who was now lowering the gun to the ground.

"It was theirs," Emeka said with pompous sincerity and settled down on a multicoloured mat that was moist and tattered. "But now it is ours. It is mine. I will use it to kill at least 100 Nigerian soldiers. What did we do to deserve all this? I don't think Zik is as wise as some of us think."

"It seems you have begun to hang around old people like me," Ngozika's mother said with a caricaturish grin of a clown. "Where did you pick up Zik and all these political news that amuse me?"

Udoka returned from the bedroom doorway and went to her grandmother to hold her hand. "Mama, enough. Enough, please. Bathe first. Go and bathe. Let me lead you to your bathroom?"

"What is a bathroom?" the old woman asked, turning to retire into the bedroom. "Bathroom? Bathroom? Perhaps it is a place where people cook?"

Emeka laughed, and Udoka turned to glare at the boy. Ngozika left them and stumbled to the window. Bats continued to explode from the roof of their obi and scatter into the young night, while others fled back into the holes. The moon had moved gently from the branches of the waving mango tree and dropped behind a red mountain. Gunshots had been replaced by the songs of blackbirds and bats. The winds, rushing into

her face through the open window, were chilly but full of sand.

She quickly drew the curtain, and something cut across her arm. Blood. It dripped from her hand onto the floor. She cleaned the blood on the curtain because it was coloured red. If the sun rose in the morning without someone—her food-hiding mother, her lizard-eating brother, her callous son, her daughter, or strangers—bringing her something to eat, it would be the second time in this war that she had gone without tasting anything.

Her brother had introduced lizards and other "unmentionables" to Emeka and Udoka, but only the boy could dare to like the meat and the other offers. This meant that the responsibility of flogging one's mind by thinking of ways to gather more food had been knocked off her shoulders. Every sunrise, Udoka had chewed the cooked green leaves that usually went to goats and never to human beings. The discoveries powered by hunger, Emeka had called his sister's eating of familiar leaves.

The last thing Ngozika had eaten was the *abacha* her mother had left under her spring bed because it reminded her of white hair "which Ojukwu luckily lacks," but "he is handling Nigeria, our enemy, with the wisdom of an old man." Her mother had said she could not eat "anything that reminds me of our hero."

Now, she had left her children behind to stay with her mother where her brother could protect them if the Nigerians came, but she could not bear to stay another minute with her mother and her pranks.

The ghostly sounds of the winds circling with leaves around the mango tree reminded Ngozika that a dead enemy was still decomposing in her house. She got up and paced the compound like some of the actors in their collapsed church. Some said it was bombed, but Ngozika did not care, did not bother to ask and discover.

Christianity was interesting and nice sounding, but Ngozika would always prefer the traditional religion. She used to take her children to one of the very few churches in Oguta because she thought Jesus Christ was a gentleman, and his Father who art in heaven sounded like a God that answers prayers, but the traditional religion felt like a part of her, just like her kidneys and heart and blood. She could not dip her hand into herself and yank out her gods and her *chi*. All her friends (four had died, and one was missing or dead too) were unable to be talked into the Igbo traditional belief, and that was why she stopped talking to them until the Nigerian bullets found their way into their chests, into their stomachs—or whichever parts they first destroyed.

Now her only friend, the only one she knew was still alive, was the fearful Mama Idu. A woman who had witnessed so many tragedies, but their friendship was not hinged on pity. It was like an anti-depressant, the friendship, and very healthy. She took Mama Idu to the first Dibia when she wanted to know why her sister kept bearing female children and only one male child. She took Mama Idu to the yam festivals and *ofalas*. She sent Mama Idu to Ogbuide the Chief Priestess to find her son, Mark.

The angry winds attacked Ngozika with the odour of the dead body. Perhaps Mama Idu will help me, and an idea sparked in Ngozika's mind. She imagined herself running after Mama Idu, then she blinked and wondered if she actually had run after someone or were all these figments of her imagination. Or perhaps she was going mad? Whatever it was, she would rather stay here and find a way to get rid of the decomposing rapist than return to her father's house to meet her mother the "War Comedian."

She settled on a rock where her late husband used to sharpen his cutlass and knife before he died. Leaves, green and brownish, left their branches and fell on her like gifts, but she was too preoccupied with the corpse, the smell, and the trouble it posed to bother about slapping them off her arm. She closed her eyes and pictured herself and Mama Idu wearing gloves and shovelling the Fulani soldier out of the house. The cloths they tied around their mouths against the odour dropped, almost simultaneously, and Ngozika opened her eyes and realised that what had just happened was not at all reality.

She was grateful. Sniffing, spitting, then standing to go to the backyard to find a solution to the problem, she ducked when a gunshot tore through the tree and exploded in the darkened sky. She screamed and dashed into the bushes. Cobwebs and dew flew into her face as she ran. She did not run far when she found Mama Idu running towards her.

"Idu?" she asked, stopping and panting.

Mama Idu's clothes were drenched with sweat and dew. "Yes, yes," Mama Idu gasped. "Are you running away? Because I am running away. I am running to your house."

Ngozika looked back. "Are they in your house? The Nigerian soldiers?"

"Let's run to your house," Mama Idu said and grasped her hand. "We need to save your children! I have hidden mine. I mean, my sister's. Of course. I have lost mine. But I have hidden everybody. Let's go and hide your children."

Ngozika turned to walk back, but her legs buckled. She fell into the woman's arms and closed her eyes. Mama Idu lifted her, and they faced the moon.

"I think the enemy is close to my house," Ngozika said without any trace of fear. "Or just the gunshots in my ears?"

"They can't come through that side. They are still far, in the neighbouring village. But let us not take risks."

"I am serious," Ngozika said and rising again. "Emeka and Udoka are with my mother. Nobody is at home. Only the corpse. That corpse."

"Oh, that rapist," Mama Idu said, looking back. "One forgets easily these days…"

Ngozika decided to be the one holding the other's hand because she thought she was more courageous. "How can it be removed?"

"The Fulani soldier?" Mama Idu asked. She was practically running with Ngozika. The line they took seemed to have the worst of cobwebs; they went into their eyes, noses, and mouths.

"Of course, yes, it is the Fulani soldier," Ngozika replied with a hint of irritation.

"Let's get there first!"

A dog—wild or domesticated, she did not know—barked with ferocious consistency, and their speed increased. Mama Idu kept saying that it was a harmless dog, perhaps a missing dog belonging to a son of Oguta, but she did not stop running. Ngozika lost her sandals while running after Mama Idu and into the darkest side of the night.

Part II

Only the dead have seen the end of the war.

- GEORGE SANTAYANA

6.

Home to the River

Ngozika remembered when she had not imagined that there would be war in Oguta. It had been a sunny afternoon. Mama Idu was not busy at home, so she had followed Ngozika to her farm.

"I hear that Nigeria was not involved in the First World War," Ngozika had said, as they harvested cassava.

"I don't know about wars," Mama Idu said. "And I don't want to know about wars. It scares me, war."

"Nothing scares me," Ngozika said. Mama Idu threw some cassava into the heap they had gathered.

"Nothing scares you, of course."

"But I shudder whenever I read Ernest Hemingway."

"I wish I could learn how to read like you."

"You speak as if you did not receive your primary education with me."

"Ngozika, we stopped at primary school, a huge accomplishment, but all fingers are not equal. Your brain is exceptional. You should be in a white man's country, and not in Oguta."

"As I was saying, I shudder wherever I read Ernest Hemingway."

Mama Idu helped Ngozika to uproot a stubborn cassava. "Why? Well, do not tell me anything about books or war. Let's talk about music, the only thing I know how to do."

"Sing," Ngozika said and laughed.

Mama Idu showed her a mock frown. "Why are you laughing?"

"I am not laughing."

"Sorry. Why were you laughing? Why, Ngozika? Was that to show that I cannot sing? You were laughing because I have not become famous."

Seriousness fell over Ngozika. "Of course, you are the most talented singer I have ever seen in Oguta. I think your talent is from the river. Sing more, dance more. Do not relent."

Mama Idu relinquished a cassava she had just uprooted, giggled at Ngozika who was going to a mango tree to get their bags for the cassava, and burst into a song.

I am glad that we are women of Biafra,

Women of Biafra,

Women of Biafra,

I am glad that we are women of Biafra.

When others have fled,

Are you a woman of Biafra?

Women of Biafra,

Women of Biafra,

Are you a woman of Biafra,

Like me and my friend?

Ngozika clapped. "Impressive," she said. "I love the melody, but it lacks substance. It is not profound. Improve the lyrics."

"Leave it like that," Mama Idu said with a laugh.

"I can't leave it like that!"

"Because you are not a coward? Because you are not a coward like me?"

Ngozika chuckled. "Yes, maybe. "

"I wish my husband had bought a piano for me before he died. I would have learnt how to play it."

"But you can play with nyo and ogene?"

Mama Udu smiled. "Yes. But I also want to practise playing white men's musical instruments."

"White women's musical instrument," Ngozika said with a frown.

"Women invented all those instruments, Ngozika?"

"Sing another song for me. A happy song. A happier song."

Mama Idu took a flute from her small handbag and blew it. Ngozika noticed that it was the song her friend had just sung, and so she supplied the lyrics. This, her incredible ability to recollect all the words, clearly

amazed and delighted Mama Idu. They sang and discussed music until the sun went down.

As Ngozika thought about her time with Mama Idu, tears filled her eyes. A talent was here, but everybody was at war. Perhaps the war would take her friend, and the world would not witness her greatness. She went to Mama Idu's house, thinking about this, and told her that she would like her help.

"What do you want?" Mama Idu asked, brushing her teeth with a tiny toothbrush.

"The soldier in my house," Ngozika said.

"Did what?"

"You understand me, Mama Idu. You understand me perfectly."

"I thought I was a coward. No?"

Ngozika wanted to smile, but her face could not soften. She said, "Let us go."

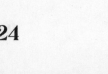

"Let me get dressed."

"But you are not naked."

Mama Idu wore her wrapper, but she went indoors to change into her red gown.

The odour of the Fulani soldier's corpse was worse when Ngozika and Mama Idu entered the house. Innumerable flies buzzed around it and the dried blood. Mama Idu screamed and ran out of the house, followed by Ngozika who covered her nose with both hands and said: "It's horrible! Ah, what are we going to do now? Do you know?"

"No!" Mama Idu said, still running into the night. Despite the circumstances, despite Mama Idu's seriousness and fear, Ngozika teased her about being a coward. Mama Idu placed both hands on her chest, trying to slow down her heavy breathing. Ngozika, too, was

breathing fast, but she did not want her friend to notice that.

And under an orange tree, far away from the house and the reek of the body, Mama Idu stopped and sat on a fallen tree. Ngozika joined her. But none of them uttered a word. The clouds above, seen through the tree branches, were lit by the stars and the moon. Here they talked about the war and children starving and dying. Ngozika said she would rather die than watch her children cry to her enemies for food as other children were doing. But Mama Idu thought that "pride is something one should relinquish in the time of war."

"Only cowards are humble," Ngozika said and looked back. An owl cried devilishly.

"It is obvious you are a heroic person." Mama Idu got up and went behind a tree to urinate, her feet crushing dead leaves. "There

is a hand here. A fallen hand. Only God knows who owns it."

"A hand?" Ngozika asked and stood. "A human hand, and just one of your fears, coward?"

"No jokes, I am serious. A hand. It is speedily decaying. Hmmm. Come and see it."

"Open the ground and bury it."

"Ngozika, be honest. Do you know who owns it?"

"Me. It's my hand."

"This is a man's hand. A huge man's man. I am not huge."

"Bury it."

Mama Idu returned with an expression of worry.

"The Goddess said that the Nigerian soldiers cannot enter into Oguta, but wasn't that the hand of one of our own?"

Ngozika sat down and picked a green leaf to crush it in her hands. "We don't know. At least I don't know. But don't be a coward. Be optimistic. I don't think they can capture us."

"Because the Fulani soldier could not capture you?" Mama Idu asked and listened. Another nocturnal bird circled the sky and cried a devilish song that was quite different from the first. Something exploded in the air, and Mama Idu gave a short scream but did not run. The winds, as though they were also frightened by the disturbance, rushed towards them, lifted their gowns, and swept the dusty floor. Then the world was silent.

"Coward," Ngozika teased again and wondered if her friend could see that her

playfulness was merely a shield to mask her trepidation. But it appeared that Mama Idu did not hear her because Mama Idu was looking behind her shoulders with undisguised fear.

A boy in soiled white clothes walked by. He carried a basket of okra, and a dog followed him closely. The red stain on his clothes sent Ngozika thinking: blood or ink? If it were blood, whose? A Nigerian soldier? She hoped fervently that it was a Nigerian soldier's blood.

"James," Mama Idu said.

Ngozika stared at her friend in confusion. "James? What do you mean, James?"

"His name is James," Mama Idu answered. "The son of Mazi Kalu."

"Who is Mazi Kalu? I don't think I remember who he is."

"Was. He is late. He was the man who hanged himself on an *udara* tree when he heard that the Nigerian soldiers had entered Oguta."

"No pity for cowards," Ngozika said and stopped. "Let's throw that corpse into the Urashi River."

Mama Idu stopped too. "A quick but wise suggestion. But I am afraid that I am not afraid. Let's go."

They turned and ran to the house. Ngozika found the big bags her husband had used to carry cassava and rice to the market when he was alive. Now she took them, and Mama Idu, whose hands were shaking terribly, helped her lift the corpse into one of the bags. Mama Idu asked, "Good, brave one. Now where? Where are we taking it?"

"To the Urashi River."

"Why?"

"Why not?"

"The river is far. We can easily throw him into a bush, can't we?"

Ngozika lifted the bag, and Mama Idu reluctantly moved closer to her to lend a helping hand. They carried the bag like a bag of rice and stumbled out of the house.

The trip to the river left them huffing and sweating, and just as Ngozika was about to make a comment about being free of the stench at last, Mama Idu shrieked. Dropping the bag, Ngozika ducked behind a shrub. But Mama Idu only stood, frozen in place.

"What—?" Then Ngozika saw it too.

Ngozika had told Mama Idu to consult the chief priestess, but she wished she had not given her friend false hope. All her confident

assurances that the missing boy would be found alive were like a wicked joke to her now.

Wailing, Mama Idu fell to her knees, and Ngozika rushed to keep her from reaching for Mark's body, floating in the river. His arms and one leg were missing as if some fish had breakfasted on them, and bullet holes were in his chest. Mama Idu sobbed into Ngozika's shoulder as they knelt in the mud beside the bag with a corpse in it.

7.

The Idea

The Idea

It was said that adolescent boys were being conscripted into the Biafran army. Mama Idu told Ngozika this with tears in her eyes as they walked on a narrow path. "But they will survive," Mama Idu added and shook her head.

"I am glad that you no longer speak like a coward," Ngozika said with a hint of satire.

"I am still a coward," Mama Idu said.

"No, you are now tough. War makes people tough. This is my observation."

"War makes people mad. This is my observation, and this is the only thing worth saying about war. It is ugly, and it makes people go crazy. Bombing and shooting at innocent children who have not eaten for weeks is the action of a crazy man, isn't it?"

"Those boys will return safe."

Mama Idu stopped to adjust her wrapper. "What makes you say this?"

"Because God is our side," Ngozika said, still walking, her slippers crushing dead leaves and rotten fruits.

Mama Idu hurried after her like a little girl. "Who are we?"

"The Biafrans. The Igbo people."

"Thank you."

"Why?"

"The idea."

"My idea?" Ngozika stopped, slapped off the grasscutter crawling on her left hand and looking at the sun, her palm a shield protecting her eyes against the sun. "When did you learn to speak cryptically?"

"Since the beginning of the war," Mama Idu said and dried her eyes on the sleeve of her black gown.

Ngozika wrinkled her face. "Can we stop speaking like teenagers?"

"I am sorry. I meant visiting these widows. It is wise. It is wise and kind. What we need now is a shoulder to lean on. Our shoulders to lean on."

A bird swooped from a tree, scooped up an earthworm, and disappeared into the sky. The elephant grass on either side of the bushes whispered in the rising winds, and the air reeked of faeces and dead things. Ngozika spat on the grass. She ignored Mama Idu, who had begun to curse Nigeria and the leaders and imagined herself throwing the nation and the entire world in which she lived into darkness.

"Let's hurry," Mama Idu said with a note of urgency.

Ngozika took her hand as though she were her daughter and not a grown friend. "We will visit Mama Oge first. That woman is good."

"Have they found her husband's corpse?"

"No, the water carried him. Nigerian soldiers are heartless."

"God will punish them."

"And burn them! They will get confused or mad and begin to kill each other."

"Please lower your voice."

"Coward."

"It is not funny."

"I know, coward."

"All those white people's novels you read are now speaking through you. You no longer talk like an Oguta woman. You no longer talk like an Igbo woman. You hid the books?"

"Only Ernest Hemingway's novels."

Mama Idu picked a crucifix from the ground. "I don't even know who he is."

"Jesus Christ?"

"No, don't be funny. I mean the name you mentioned."

"Forget it."

"Why?"

"Just forget it."

"Why, Ngozika?"

They talked like this on their way to some widows' homes. The first widow Ngozika and Mama Idu visited was a stout woman in her late forties who was named Mama Nkechi.

She was light-skinned, one-eyed, and bow-legged. Her faded green polo was torn but said IT CANNOT BE TORN. Ngozika stared at the words, read them, reread them to be sure, and thought that the words were not meant to be read literally; here was a writer trying to flaunt his or her knowledge of metaphors. But if this was metaphorical, what did TORN mean? What did IT mean? Ngozika's delayed and only answer to herself was "Igbo land." IT meant "Igbo land" and TORN meant "destroyed."

Igbo land cannot be destroyed. *Igbo land cannot be destroyed. Igbo land cannot be destroyed.* She recited this prayer in her mind three times as though she had suddenly become the chief priestess, then she coughed and looked away. Mama Nkechi waved to her skeletal daughter, Nkechi, and her blind son, Onyema, and the two children crawled into the mud house. Of course, they could walk, but one who, presumably, had not eaten for a long time could not suddenly rise and run when asked to do so. Ngozika wanted to ask their mother if she could come back with some food, or what she called food, anything at all, but Mama Idu pulled at her sleeve and nudged her. How Mama Idu read Ngozika's mind, Ngozika would never know. Perhaps one learns to predict one's friend's next action when the friendship is of age.

"Welcome," Mama Nkechi said, after offering them wooden chairs to sit on. "I am happy to see you people."

Ngozika noticed that the woman's voice, which was usually shrill and excited, had deepened, and she spoke like an elderly man who had caught a cold or was critically ill. Ngozika cleared her throat and introduced

herself and Mama Idu as if Mama Nkechi did not know them here in Oguta.

"Like I said, you are welcome," Mama Nkechi said.

"Thank you," Mama Idu said.

A cock crowed outside, and Ngozika was startled. She wondered why the bird was still alive, or perhaps her imagination was teasing her. Her imagination had begun to tease her since the day that Fulani bastard pinned her to the ground, spat into her face, and raped her. Yesterday she heard the voice of Ojukwu in her kitchen, but it was just like a lizard trapped in a pan, struggling to get out.

Perhaps that lizard, like that voice of Ojukwu, was a figment of her imagination. She sat up and said, "First of all, my friend and I are here to console you. I… we were heartbroken when we heard that the Nigerian soldiers gunned down Nnamdi, your husband, at the war front and rendered you a widow. I am a widow like you. Just like my friend Mama Idu. Things are hard. My children hardly eat. But we cannot give up. All hope is not lost. I believe in the God we serve. I believe in Chineke and my chi. Food or no food, we will triumph. This war is for us women. We should not fold our arms and watch those bloody Fulanis and Yorubas slaughter our husbands and sons like fowls. I want all the widows in Oguta to arm themselves and fight back. Cut down any enemy you see. Allow them to attack first. If you have a gun, be the first to shoot. Use any weapon in your possession. I, Ngozika cannot believe that the enemy can defeat us when we have women like you and me and Mama Idu and all the widows in this town."

Mama Nkechi grinned, and Ngozika was mildly surprised by the whiteness of her teeth. "How many guns can Ojukwu give our men? Eh? Let alone us women. We can only pray and hope. Then die or live. I am ready for the grave or the earth. Let this just end. I am tired."

"The war will end soon," Ngozika said, and a boy, or a girl—she could not tell—began to cry, like a radio powered by weak batteries. "Arm your friends and after arming yourself, then be ready to fight the enemy. The widows of the town are the town's hope."

"I like how optimistic you sound," Mama Nkechi said and opened the small wooden window to welcome the evening sun, which had turned red, going down in the east where there were many dancing trees that were reminiscent of drunk friends of Ngozika's husband. "But this is real life and not one of the stories people say you encounter in novels.

This is real life. And women mean nothing in this war. When I say *nothing*, I mean that we are not the ones who will push back Nigerians. And when I said I am tired, I don't mean that I am tired of running and screaming away from the ear-shattering sounds of bombs and guns. No, I am only saying that I am tired of waking up every day to see this beautiful sun behind us and on your beautiful faces, and then beginning to confront, every second, what it means to be alive when one does not want to be alive in a world full of dead bodies and sick children and graves of our husbands. You are better, the two of you; I have no grave to visit and dust. Your husbands have graves, but mine doesn't. I don't even know where to kneel and cry at sunset."

Ngozika stood and stumbled to Mama Nkechi who had begun to cry. Mama Idu threw a dirty but big handkerchief to Ngozika, and

she caught it in the air with the swift dexterity of a very masculine man. The sun, now half hidden by a swaying tree, continued to sink as Mama Nkechi cried in Ngozika's arms. They would dry more tears and allow more widows to cry in their arms until twilight.

This preaching—that every widow must arm herself—continued the next day. Ngozika and Mama Idu no longer moved from one house to another but now gathered all the widows on Mama Nkechi's compound and addressed them with the confidence of a Major General.

It was quite easy to use Mama Nkechi's compound because she was the last woman to lose her husband, and most women seemed to like her a lot. They circled her and tried to know if she was all right. This happened before Ngozika stood to talk. She let Mama Idu quieten the weak noises of the women before she began her speech with a nervousness that was foreign to her. She had to stop, clear her throat over and over again, and continue with fragile confidence that eventually morphed into sweaty courage and murderous rage. "Yes, we need to arm ourselves and cut off their stupid heads!" Ngozika shouted and punched the air with Mama Idu. "Men are fighting for the land, and we women, we widows, should not chicken out and hide in our houses where the enemy often discover and rape us. Some of us have been raped. Some of us will be raped. So why don't we want to take up arms and kill the Goliaths? Get knives, get cutlasses, get guns, get bombs! Get everything! Fight! Attack!"

The women shouted with frail throats and punched the air weakly. Some of them fell while trying to punch the air, and this

sent Ngozika hurrying to them to lift them from the soil that was soaked with urine. The collapse of some famished fellows, just like the ineloquence of her urgent and important speech, darkened the evening of small joys and hope, but the love that brought them together, all these women, all these widows, and their faith in her and in God's land that is Biafra, consoled and comforted Ngozika. The sun went down without any gunshots to fill the heavens, the grey heavens, and the winds were cold, but she had no one to hug. The thought of her husband made her sit up in bed and do nothing. But when the grave of the man she called husband began to hum and float to her, she screamed and ran into the night.

Later, she returned after realizing that it was just in her imagination, but she would never sleep again. She could never sleep again. She sat on the bed with her back to the peeling mud wall, Mama Idu snoring on the floor, birds twittering in trees, and she could not sleep.

8.

Enemy Territory

There was news that Owerri had been captured by the Nigerian soldiers. "But I believe that the God I serve cannot allow them to wipe out His people with those guns and those bombs," Ngozika added as she examined her gun. "Obasanjo is as heartless as he is ugly. You are shaking your head… Don't you think so? Don't you think General Obasanjo is as heartless as he is ugly?"

Mama Idu shrugged as she sat beside Mama Nkechi in her home. Mama Nkechi's children had gone into the bushes to hunt for animals and to look for firewood, so there was no other noise except the water dropping from leaves into the mud. Shifting in her chair, Ngozika nearly took a tumble because the chair was so wobbly. She got up at once to search for a better one.

Mama Idu watched her with silly laughter, but Ngozika could not decipher what the joke was. Perhaps it was because Ngozika had found a dead Nigerian soldier and stolen his gun. They had found him near the Oguta Lake, and most likely the corpse was still there, unless someone had removed it. Ngozika could not say; she stared at Mama Nkechi with all her attention. Although Mama Nkechi frowned, Ngozika knew that such a face on such an awkward occasion could not let her see what lay in her heart.

Ngozika found a good chair and now lowered herself into it. "I think it is about time we planned how to avoid death. That the Nigerian soldiers have captured Owerri means they are close to us, they are *closer* to us."

"My arms are wide open," Mama Nkechi said, peeling her decaying yam. Ngozika, who was bored and impatient, gestured to Mama Idu, and in minutes the two women walked down a lonely road.

"It may happen," Ngozika said, breaking the awkward silence.

"It will happen?" Mama Idu asked and looked at her as they walked. "Eh? What will happen?"

"Death."

"Obasanjo?"

"Don't be funny, Mama Idu. I don't mean Obasanjo. He won't die. It is people like you and me that will die. What I mean when I say it will happen is that you or I will die in this war. Or both of us. The sooner the better, in my opinion. War is not fun."

"The sooner the better?"

"Yes."

"Why aren't you sad?"

"I am sad, Mama Idu. I am sad, and that's why I want it to happen now if it is designed to happen."

Mama Idu took her hand. "It will not happen. It will not happen, Ngozika. You and I will be alive when this stupid war ends."

"You are good but cowardly. I am not saying it insultingly but honestly. Sometimes I envy you. Well, I am serious whenever I say that one of us or the two of us will die in this war. That's probability. And it is likely because we are not properly armed. The white men keep sending arms to Nigeria because they want Biafra, the stubborn Igbo people, to be obliterated or wiped out. Obasanjo may succeed, but I wish the Nigerians all the horrible things on earth."

"Where are we going to?"

"I don't know. Let us keep walking."

"And walking? And walking? No aim and no destination, Ngozika?"

"Exactly. My head is full and hot. The walk helps."

"We need guns, more guns, and then we need more willing and courageous women. Not cowards. Real women with no or minimal fears."

They moved past Chief Udo's compound and heard titled men discussing Obasanjo and the war. They were planning like the women, and this lifted Ngozika's spirit. She said, taking her friend's hand: "They impress me."

157

"Yes. They impress me," Mama Idu said, and they turned onto the road that led to Mama Idu's house. "Are we going to my house. I don't think there is any food at home."

Ngozika ignored this. "We should dig holes and cover them with palm leaves and cover the palm leaves with sand. This should be done 'round the town. 'Round our boundary."

"Why?"

"You are intelligent, Mama Idu, and I would like you to stop asking me unintelligent questions."

"You want Nigerian soldiers to drop into the holes unexpectedly?"

"And remain there until the flesh and the bones are decayed."

"This sounds nice, but I think the plan is a bit childish, and it may backfire. What if one of our people mistakenly falls into one of these imagined holes?"

"Then the enemy should celebrate, and we continue."

"I am not discouraging you."

Ngozika squeezed her friend's hand. "I know."

"You know?"

"What?"

"That you are not discouraging me."

"Then I am encouraging you?"

"Yes, maybe."

"You are mocking me, right?"

"I am not mocking your pessimism."

Mama Idu tried to laugh. "But you are encouraging my pessimism?"

"No. I am not even encouraging your cowardice."

"Discourage it, then."

"No."

"Why?"

It dawned on Ngozika that this conversation was heading towards a speedily approaching train, and she discouraged it by closing her eyes. She valued their friendship, and could not stand to see it crash. She would let the sleeping dog lie, as the English books she read had said. Let it lie. She wondered if Ernest Hemingway ever used the phrase "No," she said and opened her eyes. Mama Idu was smiling at her. She moved closer to her friend, and they hugged.

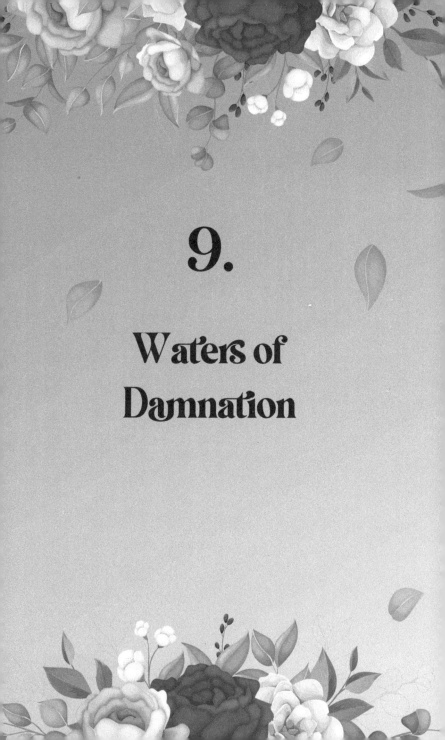

9.

Waters of
Damnation

The sun shone on the surface of Oguta Lake, glittering until a cloud crossed the sky. Gentler winds blew more than two or three hours previously, but the foul odour of decomposed bodies was nearly unbearable. The sky, a blanket of dark blue fading into greatness and gloom, was full of circling birds and clouds of smoke from the burning buildings.

No boats approached as the Nigerians rowed. Their boat was crowded with teenagers and older men who shivered not from the intensity of the cold but from unabashed trepidation. Although they had their guns, they trembled, wondering aloud if these waters were capable of a supernatural attack. Some joked about the goddess, and some were concerned.

One of the serious men was a gin-dried Yoruba soldier named Kayode Ayo. He was forty-five, but almost every fellow Nigerian who knew him thought he was much older. Perhaps it was his wrinkles and wisdom, but he was still quite healthy yet thin. Some soldiers, the insignificant minority, thought Ayo could be wiser than King Solomon. Ayo knew the truth, however; he was a coward.

Ayo spat into the lake as a white bird burst from the green bushes to cross the water. Thud. Something bumped the underbelly of their boat. "Hear am, abi?"

"The kick?" Ahmed, the muscular Hausa boy from Kano, asked. He was darker than all the northerners Ayo had seen, but he was taller and probably stronger, he assumed. Bolder.

"Yeah," Ayo replied and spat again. A bird cackled, swooping to startle them before it was gone.

Ahmed twitched to stand, then settled down. The bird dove again, and a crack broke the silence as red bloomed on the bird's breast. It dropped into the lake. But who had gunned it down? Ayo could not tell and did not bother to ask.

They were in trouble now that they'd angered the goddess of the lake, and such a question could even infuriate one of them to pull the trigger. Perhaps there was no trouble, but he liked to see this journey as such. He believed they would slaughter those Igbo bastards. He felt it with all his being, but there was a trace of fear in his heart. A bullet might hit his head from somewhere. One of them might stab him to death or throw him into

the lake. The lake itself could swallow the boat whole. This last contemplation sounded funny to him, but he was not the type who smiled often, especially not in a war like this.

"I promised my late father that I would kill one Igbo man on this Oguta Lake, but now I can't see any."

"How unfortunate!" said Timothy, a young Igala. "But we found one before."

"Where? What nameded?" a Fulani with a long nose stuttered.

"Ah...ah..." Mohammed stammered and threw something into the lake.

Mohammed's incoherence usually elicited loud laughter among his peers, but nobody laughed. Nobody even smiled. The lake was eerily silent as he glanced around, waiting for a response from the other teenagers.

Ahmed said, "My father. He died running. The Igbo people shoot him."

"You have told us this," Timothy said, tossing something into his mouth. He had the innocent face of a premature baby, but his slender frame was effeminate.

"Yes," Ahmed said with unmasked annoyance but patiently. "We heard it before? And so what? Make us keep hearing it. My father died running. They said he dey run when the Biafran soldiers' bombs—or guns—ended his life."

"This war is stupid," Ayo said and paddled faster. "Everything is foolishness. Everything we dey do. War is madness. Sorry about the loss, Ahmed."

"Thank you," Ahmed answered with arrogant indifference, gasping when the boat

danced drunkenly on the waters. "But nawa o!"

A sudden angry gust caught the exclamation and roared over it. It was magical, the speed of the winds, and the screams of soldiers who were now struggling to stay in the boat deafened Ayo. The boat tilted, sinking fast from the back. What has happened? Ayo cried in his mind because the wind was too powerful. A mysterious splitting of the wood or witchcraft—but the boat was sinking.

"Allah! Allah, save me, please!" Ahmed cried, and the water swallowed his feet and drenched his ash-green khaki.

Ayo threw himself into the lake as the boat was engulfed by the grumbling waters.

10.

Stories and Flights

10

Stories and Visions

Ngozika stumbled out of the zinc bathroom constructed outside her husband's house and saw Mama Idu coming to meet her. It was a chilly Sunday morning, and leaves from trees were falling with dew and wings of insects. The world was noiseless, except for the cheeps of the chicks that had lost their mother. This temporary peace calmed Ngozika's nerves, but the unexpected appearance of her friend scared her. She did not know why. Perhaps Mama Idu was here, this morning, to inform her that someone—a child, an adult, or a stranger—had died of hunger in her house, or could it be the Nigerian unrelenting bombings, unrelenting gunshots? Whatever it was, Ngozika knew that it must be bad news. She just knew because Mama Idu's relatively young face was now wrinkled with worries.

Or could these undesirable lines across the approaching face be an indication that these hard times were really hard times? Oh no, Ngozika thought with a forced smile. I am thinking too much. Ngozika, stop.

"Good morning, Ngoo," Mama Idu said as Ngozika gave her the conventional semi-hug. "I hope you and the children woke well. How are they? The children, I mean."

Ngozika heaved when her friend disentangled herself from the embrace. "Hunger has not killed them, but they are not here. Is everything all right? I can't remember you visiting us this early in the past. Who died?"

"Ah!" Mama Idu said, amazed and offended. "You spoke like a character in a novel. Direct and insensitive. Nowadays you

172

speak like your Ernest Hemingway novels, although I have not read one."

"And you, my friend, now have the courage to call me out. Very uncharacteristic. I am glad that your cowardice is fading away now. Is it the war?"

Mama Idu gave Ngozika a weak smile and turned her face to the house. "The war does not conquer cowardice. No war conquers cowardice."

Ngozika gently hit her red bucket on the ground to shake off the water-soaked sand that had glued itself to it. "War does not conquer cowardice, Mama Idu? You do not know what you are talking about."

"Wait," Mama Idu said.

Ngozika stopped. "What?"

"I have come with good news. "

"Good news?"

"Yes, Ngo." Ngozika waited for her to draw in a deep breath before Mama Idu blurted, "Did you hear Uncle Freddie came through the village yesterday?"

"Why should I care if Frederick Forsyth visits?" she snapped. "Can he give us something to fill our bellies? Did he give the Biafrans weapons to fight the Nigerian soldiers?"

"He will tell our story… He is our Hemingway." There was so much hope in Mama Idu's voice that Ngozika regretted talking to her so sharply, even if the woman was a coward.

"You must tell your own story. You are Hemingway." She shifted the bucket's handle in her hands. Wasn't there news? I hope that's not it, Ngozika thought. "Is that why you have come?"

Mama Idu's eyes gleamed in the sunlight. "No, there's more."

Ngozika lowered her bucket on the step and imagined Mama Idu among widows sharing bread and water. Then she dislodged the thought and said, "What's the news? The good news."

"Our prominent Oguta lady, Flora Nwapa, has arranged for a helicopter to airlift us women out of Oguta and take us to Ivory Coast, where there is a plane waiting to take us to Portugal."

"You are kidding, Mama Idu?"

Mama Idu shook Ngozika with both hands. "Believe me! Stop being pessimistic!"

The word, pessimistic, was said in English, and not in Igbo. It was one of the big words Mama Idu picked from the lips of Ngozika.

Ngozika said, "That's good news indeed."

"We need to get ready for this golden opportunity."

This plan, this golden opportunity, was also one of the things Mama Idu had learned from Ngozika. This fast learner had begun to pay a closer attention to Ngozika's English vocabulary and intonation, which was funny, but Ngozika would not laugh. She whose house is on fire does not chase rats.

Picking up the broom nearby, she swept the floor before sitting near her bucket. She did not speak as she watched Mama Idu.

"What is the matter?" Mama Idu asked and looked back at the rising sun. "Look, Ngo, we need to prepare and prepare fast. Opportunity, you say, waits for no one."

176

"I don't know how to get this news across to my brain," she said and put her head into her hands.

"I would like him to help me. I want to take my children along. But I am afraid. The road leading to the house is dangerous. Nigerian soldiers are raping and killing our women."

Mama Idu squatted, and Ngozika perceived a faint smell of crayfish. "You are afraid? I did not know that you could be afraid. God this war is draining me. Stand up. Please."

But Mama Idu did not stand. She only lifted her head, her eyes heavy with tears, and she watched the sun leaving the blue-grey clouds that had eclipsed it. Ngozika followed her stare as several eagles hovered.

Part III

Part III

There is no avoiding war; it can only be postponed to the advantage of others.

- NICCOLO MACHIAVELLI

11.

Land of Hunger

The evening sun was sinking into the dark clouds when Ngozika found Mama Idu near a crowd and told her that she planned on going to Ogwuma. She said it in English first, then remembering Mama Idu's English was hilariously poor, she translated her words immediately.

"Ogwuma?"

"Ogwuma," Ngozika replied, "yes. I want to get my children, Mama Idu."

Mama Idu stepped away from the crowd to understand why Ngozika needed to return to her village. Ngozika had no supernatural powers to read minds, but she could see that what she had concluded was the truth.

The crowd was mostly made up of younger and middle-aged men and three dogs.

Fleetingly Ngozika wondered why the three animals were still alive in a land of hunger, then returned her attention to the crowd. Mama Idu's eyes were also on the crowd. Most of the sympathizers who had gathered before this present group dispersed shaking their heads. The women among them cried and wailed. Some of them even rolled on the ground like characters on a stage.

The reason for this convergence was loud in the air: Nigerian soldiers raped yet another Igbo girl, beheaded her, and threw the body into the lake for it to cross the lake into the bushes. The mother of the decapitated girl was a white-haired woman named Grace. Her daughter, the one whose head was dipping blood and in her shaking hands, was also named Grace. And she wailed. The women cried too. There was one slender man who was so fair Ngozika wondered if he was an albino: he was the only man who cried.

"Her only daughter," one limping elderly woman commented in a mournful tone and turned to leave. "Her only daughter."

"Her only child, in fact," Ngozika said, as though she had given Ngozika this information before they both hurried to this market square to witness a woman with the bloody head of her daughter, her only child. Her husband, a Biafran soldier who had died the month the war began, had been Mama Idu's first husband.

Ngozika stepped out of the gathering and said, "The sun is going down."

"Her only child," Mama Idu mourned and allowed herself to be kindly and gently dragged to a mango tree by Ngozika.

"I need to get my children," Ngozika said. "And I must leave tonight."

Because she had resolved to make the journey to Ogwuma tonight she wore a black sweater and black boots. In a light or jolly situation, she would have found her appearance funny, but this was war, and her children must be found. There were limited spaces on board the helicopter, and her family had to be on it.

She followed the perimeter of the backyard with birds singing in trees and insects flying into her face. Wiping a leaf from her cheek, she walked toward the main road. By the time she appeared on the major road where a bus, a lorry, or any vehicle that could carry her to Ogwuma would be found, it was almost late. The moon had appeared above, partially swallowed by black swirling clouds of grey smoke, and Ngozika wondered if the surreal picture above was real or perhaps hunger and sorrows had worsened her sight.

She imagined a slowly flying bird with feathers of primary colours and a better sky, one so blue and white in parts, and she found herself closing her eyes to savour this image. Perhaps she was losing her mind; she just wanted to escape, to find herself in a different world, in a different body. A gunshot rang out some distance away, reminding her she was exposed to danger on this road. She hastened, her boots scratching the rough earth, and all she could think of were her children.

She used to tell them teasingly that they were all characters in her eyes, all Ernest Hemingway's characters, but she did not tell them why she thought so. She did not even know why she always thought so. The

search for her children, the best boots she was wearing, the war and the hunger it brought, the constant temptation to take her life—they all reminded her of Ernest Hemingway. Did this great man of letters know about Nigeria? About Igbo people? About the things that were wrong with Africa and Africans?

Would he like her if he saw her in the other world? Would he like to put her in one of his war-themed novels if he magically appeared on this road? Perhaps he would walk past her without saying a word after admitting that a white man could not tell an African story for the African. Perhaps it would be a good idea if she wrote about this man? And in the story, she thought and rolled up her sleeves, I will not let my children get lost. God, I will not let my children get lost. God, I will not let my children get lost.

But her heart was heavy, and her feet were weak. She might fall if she ran again or tried to run. Birds were busy with their songs and whistling, and there was still no human being in sight. Even animals. God, I will not let my children get lost. I will not let my children get lost. I will not let my children get lost.

She shouted inside her head, like a lunatic, but her feet were weak. And as the first tear dropped in the grass, she looked back and saw that the distance she would walk to get home was almost as long as the distance she would walk to find a vehicle. She dried her eyes on her sleeve and continued to trudge with very little hope, the stars and the moon her torches and only company.

12.

Vandals in the Homeland

The stench of faeces and carcasses hung in the air, flies buzzed everywhere, and insects twitched in the whistling bushes. Ngozika slapped a noisy bee away from her face and hastened her steps. The wind rushed into her open mouth, but she did not want to close it. It was her worst habit, drinking the air.

As a kid, she would escape into the morning and circle the house with her mouth wide open, and now it was not just a habit, she needed it. Her legs trembled, from exhaustion or hunger, she did not know, but to give up was to accept death. She only stopped to pluck her peeling black leather sandals from her feet, removed a pebble, and continued her run.

The voice of her waiting children followed her, but she knew it was just in her imagination. A horrible host of owls screeched, causing her to lose one of her sandals. There was no need to keep the other one, so she let go of it and took the wilder road by her left and into wet cobwebs. "My God!" She said and fell into yellowing cassava leaves.

She shook the dust from her gown as she scrambled to her feet. "Oh, God!" she exclaimed in English, growing more frightened by the minute. The thought of a Nigerian soldier, a rapist, or a beastly person hiding behind these quivering leaves kept her legs shaking.

Her feet had not been silent, and she'd cried out in English, the language understood by the enemy, and she was not armed, except the knife the Yoruba soldier

had given her. A knife could not defend against a bullet. Why did she encourage all the Oguta widows to arm themselves with guns and other dangerous weapons when she could not use hers consistently? There was no time to reprimand herself for her careless forgetfulness. But who could possibly have the luxury of time in matters of grave urgency and sole opportunities? She must keep going, armed or not.

The moonlight gleamed as the roof-shaped branches of trees retreated, and she heaved. The ground had been lit, but the first thing that caught her eyes and tore her heart was the butchered body of a pregnant woman. She had lost her hands, one leg, and her stomach was torn open with the foetus like a dead animal collecting blue-coloured flies and strange insects.

The odour hit her nose as the winds slapped her face. But she did not scream, for it did not hurt her heart or make her feel paralysed. This revived stoicism was quite surprising to her but utterly consoling. Out of the bushes and down the sensibly wide road that led to Ogwuma and (God, please!) to her children, Ngozika emerged. Her eyes were full of cobs and leaves and dew, but she was grateful for this thinly expected achievement of proximity. But hardly had she cleaned her eyes and opened them did the most traumatising spectacle confronted her sight.

Nigerian soldiers, whom she had been avoiding, ran on the road ahead. Fifty to eighty of them, killing and maiming Oguta men, women, children, and animals. Some of the soldiers shouted, "Allahu Akbar!" as they sliced the Igbo with machetes. Many killed without uttering a word, but they carried matches and knives. Their guns shone, and maybe they had other weapons well concealed.

Ngozika scrambled back into the bushes, peeking through the leaves, waiting until they passed to find another route to Ogwuma.

13.

This Night is Different

Her village, at night, was a perfect eerie silence, but whenever there was tragedy or someone important died, the people—especially women and children—raised their crying voices in solidarity. But this night when Ngozika returned seemed different.

The oldest man in the village, Mazi Ibekwe, had fallen to his face after the bomb blast; the newborn twins, Anya and Zoba, had closed their eyes for good after days of starvation and hopelessness; a pastor had overdosed in a church after writing a short letter to God. Although Ngozika had learned of all these misfortunes from the chatty driver she had flagged down on the road, no one in town was talking about this when she arrived. It seemed to her that everyone had become so used to this adversity that the subject of obituaries seemed fruitless and depressing, tedious and irritatingly pretentious. What constantly proved honest and refreshing was the topic of sick elderly people and missing folks and missing children.

After Ngozika had seen the soldiers on the road, she had waited until the marchers passed, then scurried home to find another way. She had caught a ride with a speeding driver, but the sun had not yet risen when she arrived outside her home. There were five men gathered in her yard.

When she walked toward them, she heard her brother's name on their lips. She missed him dearly, having not been able to visit as much during this war. The eldest one among the men grumbled, rubbing his balding head, "Yes, I heard Chikwado has been killed by the Nigerians this afternoon."

Ngozika's heart dropped. "What's that?" She rushed closer, but the men received her with lazy and awkward greetings. "Who died, please?" she asked Ichie Chukwukere, a man in his forties who sat on a mat. His wife had recently died during the birth of their sixth child.

Two of the five men shared the same name—Nnaemeka—and they were friends. Short and dark, big noses—one was playfully called Senior, but at forty-one he was younger. Junior was forty-eight. Both men were fishermen, and many called them twins. They were listening to Mazi Peter, a big-eyed man in glasses, speak about how it was actually the Northerners who started the "senseless" war.

Ngozika had heard this sentiment before; she only wanted to hear about her brother but held her tongue.

"Yes, I agree," Junior said, and Ngozika stepped closer. "Northern soldiers—I mean, the fight was not against Northern people but against those corrupt men. Most of these people in charge are Northerners. Did they expect our soldiers to kill innocent people instead?"

"Please, I heard something," Ngozika tried to make her voice heard, but Senior spoke over her.

"Junior, what a way to look at it."

Junior said, "Let us leave all these men. I think it is proper if we inform Ngozika about this loss."

She stifled a gasp. "Which loss?" she asked, hoping that what she heard, what was obvious, would in the end prove to be a drunken joke that men were about to toughen

her with. But it was not a joke because Ichie Chukwukere frowning.

"We found his body in the bushes. It happened," he repeated and lifted his head gloomily. "The young man died in Owerri." He wiped the sweat from his forehead, eyes gazing at the sky as if remembering. "No, it was here. It was not in Owerri, of this I am sure now. I remember it. How sad it is. It was your brother who was conscripted into the army in Owerri."

"In Umuahia," Peter corrected.

Why was he not in Ogwuma with my children? Ngozika thought as her shoulders dropped. She placed both hands on her head in despair and took off running, screaming all the way. The men ran after her, except Ichie Chukwukere who sat down. It was sunrise when they found her seated on a broken chair

in an abandoned church, sobbing and shaking. She was not here to pray, just to hide from the world, but the men thanked God for saving her before taking her home.

14.

Tidings of the Missing Children

Since Ngozika had returned to her husband's house, she had heard troubling rumours. Not only was her brother found dead, but it seemed that Emeka may have been conscripted into the Biafran army. But rumours were not always facts, although she hoped it was true. After all, it was better that one stayed alive to fight the enemy than to lie motionless in some smelly bush, decomposing like hundreds of other bodies.

It was a sunny afternoon, but she was in bed, imagining her children dead and wondering why God had not chosen to wipe out Nigeria and her evil soldiers and citizens. Beside her on the bed was a dog-eared copy of *The Old Man and the Sea*. She had not read it since the war began, but she used to read it almost every six months. Now, all she could do was stare at the cover with the writer's name staring at her.

Although the author's name was Ernest Hemingway, the person who pirated it had written, 'Earnest Hemingway.' She had forgiven the misspelling, but the other book, The Sun Also Rises, which she had read, was pirated hilariously by an amateur or a joker. On this book, the author's name was spelled,'Ernest HemMingway' with a double "m." Who could do this? A madman, perhaps. Or a mad woman. Ngozika opened the book to read a paragraph on page 56:

Now I will pay attention to my work, and then I must eat the tuna so that I will not have a failure of strength.

She could not read further because her eyes were blurry with tears of frustration, hopelessness, and hunger. "I must eat the

tuna," Hemingway had written for himself and people like her, but she could not eat any fish. She could not eat any fish because she could not find any fish. The lake and the rivers were dangerous. Nigerian soldiers lurked there, or so the stories went. A voice in her head urged her to fling the novel to the wall and go look for her missing children, but her insides felt hollow and empty. She would faint if she tried to stand.

Rising winds threw the broken wooden door open, but she was not startled. She had become used to sudden winds, sudden screaming, and sudden death. But sudden abductions of children? What about missing children? No, no, her children were not missing; they were with someone they all knew. Or maybe the five bald men who had welcomed her helped the children escape to Umuahia to hide and to survive. The bombings

and killings had become unbearable in Oguta, and many locals were escaping to Umuahia.

But if she could not find her children, she would not escape on her own on the helicopter that was rumored to be arriving soon.

A fowl flew into the house through the window, and she rushed with arms high to scare it back outside. But the earth-shaking sounds of bombs sent her screaming out of the house.

Men, women, and children ran helter-skelter, and the clouds were filled with fire and grey smoke. They all screamed as they ran, and Ngozika hurried after them with incredible agility. Halfway in the bushes, she spotted Ichie Chukwukere.

The coward, as she liked to call him, was on the back of his son Udo, a teenager

with the strength of a well-fed adult and the wisdom of an elder. Ngozika did not only accept these admirable qualities because the villagers thought they were apt but from her own interactions with him. She used to fantasize about introducing the lad to Ernest Hemingway, but the war had dashed that. She was close enough to see that Ichie Mazi Chukwukere had dislocated his leg and bruised his ankle. The bandage around his ankle was bloody, and he shamelessly shed tears. It usually annoyed her, shedding tears, especially men shedding tears in public, but she could not reprimand them.

"Ichie Chukwukere!" Ngozika called, tearing the last cassava leaf out from her face and stumbling closer to Ichie Chukwukere. Ngozika stumbled closer to Udo and his father. The one who carried the other should come first irrespective of the age, of the time.

"Ichie Chukwukere!" Ngozika asked again, breathless and oddly excited.

But it was Udo who answered. "Good evening, Sister. Ichie Chukwukere is wounded, as you can see. I know you are genuinely sympathetic, but there is no time to spare. Let's go! Let's run! Let's run this way…"

Udo tried to run, but he fell into a bush of buzzing insects, and Ngozika helped them get back on their feet.

"Thank you," Ichie Chukwukere told Ngozika and began to limp beside his son. "Thank you, Udo. You have been so good and so kind. Ngozika, my daughter, I thank you again. Help me thank the Lord for giving me a child like Udo. I was shot at the market square—Nigerian soldiers are everywhere, you know. He treated me like a Red Cross doctor would do. And now we are going to my wife's father's village to continue hiding from the bombs, and of course postpone our death. Where are you going? Just asking as we are both confused. I don't even know where to go, which road to take, and when the enemy will attack. But where are you going to?"

"Me?" Ngozika asked, following them.

"I forgot to tell you that your missing children are not missing," Ichie Chukwukere said.

Ngozika gasped. "What? What do you mean? Where are they, please?"

"Dad, stop talking, please." Udo yanked up the leg of his pants to keep the fabric from dragging in the dirt. "Remember what I told you."

"Yes, I do," Ichie Chukwukere said and lapsed into silence.

"I am sorry, Sis," Udo said.

"What?"

"I am sorry."

"Stop being sorry! What do you mean? What does your father mean?"

Ichie Chukwukere coughed wildly as if he wanted to shush his son. "Stop shouting. No quarrels. I will explain…"

"Your leg, Papa," Udo said, grasping his father's hand. "Your leg and your health. You have not even eaten anything. Kindly hold your tongue. Thank you."

"Ngozika." Ichie Chukwukere coughed.

"Yes?" Ngozika slowed her pace because the injured man could not hurry.

Udo said, "Daddy?"

"Ngozika, your children are safe. Chief Nnanna took them to Umuahia. They were on his bus."

Ngozika rushed to seize the man in confused fury, but she stepped back in a mixture of anger and sadness. The man slumped and rolled down to a hollow path littered with grass. His eyes ceased to blink. Udo dropped to his knees and looked back at her with tears in his eyes as though she could raise the dead to life. Udo and Ngozika stayed frozen in shock until the sharp gunshots nearby galvanized Ngozika and Udo to carry the man home and bury him. But could they do this without being shot or bombed?

Udo shook the lifeless man, crying and begging him to answer, or Udo would join him in the other world. Ngozika twitched. I cannot wait here. I must find my children

in Umuahia, she thought. "Let's go. We must bury him." She scooped the dead man's legs in both of hers, and Udo went to his shoulders.

15.

Holy Pagan

Ngozika leaned against the window on the last bus to Umuahia. The driver was shirtless and shiny with sunlit sweat, and about sixty other Oguta people and other Igbo people chattered noisily around her in other seats. Beside the driver stood the 'conductor,' a smelly old man in ragged jeans. He was armed with a gun and a dagger and chewed atu osisi, passing some to the driver. Both men loudly cursed General Obasanjo and Nigeria as the bus sputtered through swirling clouds of dust.

He drove carefully, but Ngozika loathed him. The man was avuncular and encouraging all through the journey, but when he braked to allow a car to pass at an intersection, he said, "Some of us will die in Umuahia."

This heartless pessimism shocked and needled Ngozika. She rose with her small leather bag and knife and said, "Thank you, Driver, but watch your tongue. It is wicked. And learn to wash. Let me off here."

"I am sorry," the driver said, blinking in astonishment. "My dear, you interpreted my words wrongly. I did not mean to hurt us, but this is the truth. This is the sad truth. Some of us will die in this city." Regardless, he screeched to a stop.

"I will not die," a middle-aged woman in a filthy white gown said as she stumbled out of the bus with Ngozika. Other women also rebuked the driver, and some cursed him. The men among them tried to quiet the women, but Ngozika left them, shaking her head. She would not allow him to curse her when she was so close to reuniting with her children. She was not sure if she could still make it aboard the helicopter Mama Idu told her about, but she had to try.

She walked for an hour until she reached the outskirts of Umuahia, but where did the chief take her children? Perhaps someone would know.

The first place she stopped was a church. A Catholic church, judging by the statues of the Blessed Virgin Mary and Jesus Christ on the Cross of Calvary that flanked the entrance. Burnt and broken, the church had seen better days, but it was still recognizable. The name of the church was covered with grey smoke, and the floor, cemented and painted green, had been filled with burnt branches.

Ngozika scrunched her nose at the odor of dead things. Not human beings, perhaps, but definitely dead things. Of course, she

thought, the church witnessed a number of dead Biafrans, but one would assume they had been removed and buried.

Two young men were coming out of the church when Ngozika sat on the pavement to rest and plan. One of the men—the shorter and darker one—sobbed, telling the other that the air raids had not targeted his family, of course, but it seemed that they did. He had lost his father in the church, his mother, his two brothers, and two sisters, and he was the only one of his family left in the world.

"Ikechukwu," the taller one said, putting a consoling hand on the man's shoulder. "God knows the best, Ikechukwu, I said God knows the best. Be a man, Ikechukwu. It is well. It is well, Ikechukwu. Remember that you are not a woman, Ikechukwu."

226

"I am hopeless," Ikechukwu said, stumbling beside his friend.

"Ikechukwu," his friend called again.

Ngozika frowned as they walked past her and onto the lonely road that smelled of blood and danger. She had never hated any human being who was trying to console the bereaved, but she found herself hating this very young man in a faded black polo and ripped jeans that were spattered with mud. Perhaps her hate stemmed not from the histrionic way in which he repeated the sobbing friend's name as though the man had forgotten his name in his mourning, and he was trying to remind him. Perhaps it stemmed from the speaker's encouragement which was also an inference that it was women, and not men, that were expected to shed tears and show vulnerability.

He must be a goat, Ngozika concluded. His brain is weak. A goat's weak brain.

She watched them until they thinned in the distance, and she got up and yawned. Stretching, she found no strength left in her, and she sunk back down onto the concrete. There was nothing to eat in her bag, and she could not imagine hunting with a knife on weak legs. On the road, there were a group of stick-like children with protruding bellies trudging with bowls and sticks. Only God knows what they are searching for, she thought, and only God can help them now.

Nigerians kept dropping bombs, and Britain kept sending ammunition to Nigeria against the Biafrans. What could she do now to help her people? What could she do to help herself first? Is it even possible to find my children now? She thought, her throat growing tight. I do not know where to look or who to ask.

She could not tell exactly why she thought so, but she believed, strongly and tearfully, that she would never find them. Nevertheless, she would keep looking for them. To fold her arms and turn back to Oguta would mean she was the personification of heartlessness, and she had always aspired to be the image of motherhood before the war.

A young man in his mid-forties with a cutlass and a Bible staggered out of the burnt church and seemed startled when he saw her.

"Oh, young lady," he said in Igbo and gave an awkward smile. He was emaciated, and his teeth were surprisingly white. Perhaps he was not from Umuahia because his dialect was different and clear.

She said, "Good afternoon."

"I am sorry that I startled you, woman," he said.

"I am sorry that I startled *you*," she said.

"What?"

"I am sorry that I startled you."

"I never said you startled me, woman."

"And I never said that you startled me, but I clearly startled you. Why have you chosen to apologize for startling someone whom you did not startle after she has startled you?"

The man smiled, and she saw that he was dimpled. "You are different. I mean, you are interesting."

"Thank you. Have you seen my children? Chief Nnanna took them to Umuahia where they might be safe."

"Nowhere is safe. My name is Emeka Okafo. I am a pastor. I lost my father in this church. The air raid killed him."

She sniffed because he smelled of smoke and plants. "I am sorry about that, but my children? Their names are—"

"What's your name?"

"I am not Pastor Emeka Okafo," she snapped, realizing he was deliberately ignoring her request for him to help with her children.

He lowered his cutlass and smoothed his Bible. "Perhaps my cutlass is frightening you. I have dropped it. See?"

"Even your gun cannot frighten me."

"I have no gun. I am a pastor, have you forgotten?"

"Pastors don't go round with guns?"

"No. God is our protector."

"But pastors can go round with a cutlass?"

Pastor Emeka Okafo sighed. "I find you tiring but interesting. Are you from this town?"

"Please go."

"I would like to share the word of God with you. I know many of us Igbo people are frustrated and depressed because of this ugly war, but God is with us, believe me." He paused to look surreptitiously at her chest and then continued in a lowered voice, "Do you believe in our Lord Jesus Christ?"

Ngozika wondered if those eyes that fell on her chest were lustful, or was that fleeting look accidental, careless? She said, "My faith is none of your business, Pastor Emeka Okeke."

"Okafo. Pastor Emeka Okafo."

"Please go. I need to stay alone. I have no place to go. My kids are missing, and I am here waiting for death to come and take me. I am tired."

"That's why you need to run to me… to Jesus. That's why you need Jesus. I am his messenger, and I keep running to him. Give Jesus a chance, Nneoma."

"Stop mistaking me for your wife."

"Oh, sorry. That's not my wife. My colleague in the lord. She was a pagan. I am not married."

Ngozika spat. "Why?"

"The war took her. Her name was Chioma. A true child of God. She was a pagan too. I converted her, and now she is happy in heaven, and she is drinking and dancing with the angels above. I am glad that I made it possible. I will make it possible for you."

"Do not make anything possible for me. No, help me. Help me look for my missing children. They were taken from Oguta and brought here in Umuahia."

Pastor Emeka Okafo lifted his cutlass. "I went hunting, but I caught nothing. But I will find your children. Maybe… No, God certainly made me fail in my hunting in order to meet you and help you find your children. Give me your hands."

She wanted to give him her hand but stopped suddenly; the man of God had an erection. She spat into his face, snatched his cutlass from him, and rose to walk away. The pastor gaped at her, saying nothing, doing nothing, as she walked away with the cutlass and her bag. All hope was lost; she would not find her kids, but she would find the head of a Nigerian soldier, or Nigerian soldiers, cut

the damn things off. She would fight Nigeria until she could not, and she could not. Let the world end if she failed to find her kids. Tears had blurred her vision, but she was still marching on the road where flies circled dead bodies of fallen Biafrans.

Part IV

If we don't end war,
war will end us.

- H. G. WELLS

16.

Looking but not seeing

After flagging down a driver, Ngozika arrived in Umuahia at last. "I do not know where your children are, but maybe the ones who live in this village have seen them. May God be with you." He seemed so cheerful despite his growling belly the whole drive.

Ngozika closed the door, adjusted the cutlass in her belt, and walked to three little boys with distended bellies. Screaming, they scrambled over one another to get away. Maybe the boys could not tell her from a Nigerian soldier. She wanted to yell, "Nigerians have guns! Now help me find my children!" but what was the point? The boys had vanished between two homes.

243

A woman stepped out of her door, eating a rotten yam, but when she saw Ngozika, she returned inside and slammed the door. Ngozika glanced at the cutlass at her side. If I want anyone to speak to me, I will need to get rid of this weapon, she thought. She thought of the knife the soldier had given her. It was better than no weapon at all.

Kneeling beside a bush, she hid the cutlass in the tall grass. Hopefully, she would be able to remember where she had hidden it when she found her children. She wandered through the village until she came upon a group of thin, balding men. They did not run as she approached. "Can you help me? I am looking for my children; Chief Nnanna brought them here in his bus."

244

"Chief Nnanna?" The tallest of the men shook his head. "No. We have not seen his bus in weeks."

"Weeks?" Ngozika's stomach clenched. "No, this cannot be. He was on his way here a few days ago."

"No, not here. Sorry."

"Wait, what are your children's names?" the man with three missing teeth asked.

"Emeka and Udoka. Have you seen them?" There was a frantic energy buzzing in Ngozika's words, but she did not know where the energy had come from.

"Emeka… Emeka… Was that the boy that was conscripted?" He scratched his head.

"Yes, I think he was. That was three days ago," the tall one said.

"What about my daughter? Udoka?" Ngozika was breathless. How could her son have been conscripted?

"No, I do not think I remember her." The men shook their heads, exchanging glances with each other.

"Oh no," Ngozika gasped. "I will never find my children now!" She stumbled down the road into a field. Hands on her headscarf, Ngozika wailed into the night. She stood beneath the bruised clouds, throwing back her head to scream. Before the war, she prided herself on being a great mother. What was she now? She was alone, and the helicopter would leave them all behind. There would be no safety for her or anyone in her family.

Wobbly-kneed, Ngozika squatted over a stone. That frantic energy that had kept her moving all day had left her in an exhale. I am

starving, my children are gone, and there is no hope in finding them, Ngozika thought. She plucked a blade of elephant grass and tore it into pieces. Being depressed helps no one, and in war, everyone loses family, Ngozika thought.

Could the rumors be wrong? Her children might still be safe, somewhere far from here.

Ngozika bit her lip, bringing her back to the present. The Nigerians had stolen her family from her with their war. "I know where the Biafran soldiers camp beside the lake," she blurted, although there was no one to hear her. As quickly as she could walk, she rushed back to where she had stored the cutlass and dug it out of the grass. "I am going to destroy as many Nigerians as I can." Maybe the soldiers would not be able to help her find her children, but they were not cowards.

17.

A Searing Search

Ngozika joined the Biafran soldiers on a Saturday afternoon. The sun was scorching, and she imagined the back of her neck dissolving like congealed groundnut oil. But she was not discouraged, not tired, not hopeless. She was hungry but determined to find her children in this town. If her son was conscripted by the Biafrans, he would be here, and he would know where his sister was hiding.

One soldier took interest of her search when she did not find her son among them, and the soldier was an enormous Oba man named Major Ifechukwu Okafor. She had stumbled upon him, bellowing to the sky, "If you help the Biafrans win the war, God, I, Major Ifechukwu Okafor, will worship and praise Him until I breathe my last on Earth."

Together, the pair stood outside a thatch-roofed restaurant where many Biafran soldiers and their friends came to eat roast plantains. Already, the moon shone in the deep indigo sky, and the last gleams of sunlight fell behind the hills and waving palm trees. The winds were alive with rage, and the dust rose, swirling high above her head, with some settling on the branches of the palm trees that surrounded this restaurant. Dust clawed Ngozika's eyes, and she hurried into the restaurant after the Major.

As Ngozika entered, every soldier instinctively reached for their guns which were lying on the mud floor, but they waited for Major Ifechukwu's order. Breathless, Ngozika waved. "Daalu," she said in Igbo, and the men dropped their weapons with a short laugh.

The men all around her spoke in Igbo, but the lone, "Feel at home," was in English, making Ngozika wonder if they were trying to impress her. She sat on the bamboo chair facing the major and another man when the cook asked her what she would like to eat.

"Honestly, I would like to eat, but I have no money," she answered.

"So why are you here?" snapped Major Ifechukwu. He was high skinned with feminine, slender fingers, but his voice was deep, unfriendly, and unattractive.

She visualized him strangling an infant, then stopped and said, "I am tired, sir. I am tired of walking. I was looking for my son, but he is not here. Can I rest her for a minute if I cannot eat something?"

"Interesting," the proprietor said with a contagious grin, and she saw some of his

teeth were missing. He was thin and haggard in his khaki. The offensive odor of cigarettes emanated from him. Ngozika wondered what his name was, why he chose to cook for his colleagues, and how he succeeded in getting into the Biafran army.

"Are you married? Major Ifechukwu asked, his bloodshot eyes hit with undisguised lust.

Ngozika restrained herself from shaking her head. An ugly man with an uglier attempt at flirtation, she thought, but in English she said, "Impressive pick-up line, sir. But yes, I am married."

Major Ifechukwu frowned and turned to his colleague. "Isn't her confidence charming, Udoka?"

Udoka? So this was the man's name? It reminded Ngozika of her late husband's

friend, and effeminate dancer also named Udoka who had died before the war began. He had no wife, no son, no daughter, no remarkable achievement. He owed a lot of people, including women. Ernest Hemingway would not like to open a character like this.

"You seem distracted," Udoka told her. "What is the matter, beautiful woman?" He asked the question with a smile, but there was no trace of lust in his voice.

"I lost my kids," Ngozika said and burst into tears that surprised and embarrassed her. "I lost my kids."

Major Ifechukwu dipped his hand into his pocket and brought out a cigarette. "Which kain woman be this?" he asked in pidgin English and lit the cigarette with a lighter.

Udoka rushed toward her with popping eyes. "Wetin happen? Wetin happen?"

"Not lost, really," she said in English, then switched to her rural Igbo. "They are missing. There are two of them—a boy and a girl. They are missing. They are missing. They are missing…"

Major Ifechukwu interrupted her. "I thought you were pretending to be a man, acting tough and stoic. They are missing. They are missing." The last sentences were said in Igbo in Ngozika's accent to ridicule her. But she was too weak, too hungry, and too sad to attack back. What she needed now was not a fight with a soldier but to eat and drink and look for her children.

"What really happened?" Udoka asked her, coming to squat beside her.

The loving tenderness of Udoka's voice compelled Ngozika to wipe her tears with

a handkerchief, but Major Ifechukwu lit another cigarette.

"They are safe in this town," Udoka said and went to an open cupboard where food-filled pots were kept to offer her the dinner she so craved. She lifted her face and, for the first time, scanned the restaurant.

"You want us to help you?" Major Ifechukwu asked and blew a cloud of smoke into her face.

"Stop that, please!" she said.

Major Ifechukwu did it again and chuckled. "You no dey smoke? Because you be woman, abi? Come and have a cigarette, my love. It dey funny, it dey very funny, stumbling into our place, crying and asking for food. Udoka, this woman go sweet, I swear. But you no dey like woman. Why you no dey like woman?"

"I like her," Udoka said with a smile, returning with a plate of beans and a cup of water. "If I no like her, I for no give her food and water. I like her a lot. She is a good woman, I think."

"Are you a good woman?" Major Ifechukwu asked her.

"I am a good soldier," she replied in Igbo and took the food and water from Udo. Her hands shook, and the water spilled. Major Ifechukwu laughed and lit the last surviving cigarette.

"You are a good soldier?" Major Ifechukwu asked.

"I want to be one," she said. "How can I join you people? I am serious. I am serious, and I am angry. I want to be a soldier, a Biafran soldier. Can you help me?"

Udoka looked at Major Ifechukwu with pleading eyes, and the smoker dropped his cigarette and stamped on it with his mud-coated boots. "Come with me," Major Ifechukwu said.

"Let her finish her food first, please," Udoka said.

Bombs or strange gunshots were heard in the distance, and the earth shook.

Twenty minutes later, Ngozika and Major Ifechukwu walked towards a bombed Catholic church that was surrounded by cashew trees. They stopped when they got to the gate and asked passersby—children and adults—if they saw any missing children, but they all said no and continued hurrying with their baskets and buckets. Perhaps they went to take food from charitable people at the church. Ngozika could not see the contents

of the things they carried, but she could conjecture that they were food and clothes and drugs. She mentioned her kids' names, hometown, and described their looks, but no one said they knew them or saw them. Tired and frustrated, she turned and left.

At night, she slept in the restaurant after the useless search.

The next day, Major Ifechukwu took her to the "barracks," introducing her to his colleagues, and she quickly trained (running, jumping, and practicing shooting) and was given a dusty uniform. The next day, she shot a Hausa-looking man running to a river with a tattered mat and tossed his corpse into a bush where flies buzzed.

"Did you see my son and my daughter?" she asked a group of shirtless boys in the street on her way back to the restaurant.

"No," they chorused with indifference and perhaps fear and continued walking towards the sunlight. They stopped when they heard sounds of gunshots, then continued as if nothing dangerous had happened. The winds rushing into their faces were full of sand and frost.

"Their names are Emeka and—wait, please!" she cried, but the boys did not stop. She settled on a rock and imagined a heavy rain falling on her, her head, and her shoulders, on Umuahia, and drowning everybody and carrying the dead bodies to an ocean. The images of her children stabbed her heart, and she closed her eyes. Tears trickled down her cheeks.

261

18.

Decaying Things

The time was 2:30 p.m., but the sunlight was weak and partly obscured by the dancing palm trees that surrounded the so-called barracks in Umuahia. Uniformed and not uniformed men milled around, chatting in low tones. Some of them sat under dust-coated tree-like flowers, smoking or filling their guns with bullets. Ngozika, seated at a rusty table littered with empty plates and empty bottles, shifted and frowned. The so-called barracks had become almost unbearably boring. Seated beside her at the table was Major Ifechukwu who was smoking a cigarette and talking about the group of Nigerian soldiers whom he had gunned down. But she found this boastful talk unnecessary and puerile. She faked a cough, and the pompous soldier dropped his cigarette and said sorry.

"It's okay," she said in English.

"You are distracted," he said in Igbo, and Ngozika was surprised that he chose the language and not the colonial masters' English, which usually impressed young Igbo women.

"Yes, I am distracted," she said, staring at a teenager who was walking by with a fowl. The boy reminded her of Emeka her son, and her heart sank.

"That's my son," Major Ifechukwu said and lit another cigarette. "His name is Love. It should be a girl's name and not a boy's name. I like originality. That's why I gave him the name. Love. Love. Love. I like romantic names. What's the name of your son again? But answer this question first. This one: Do you love Love? Not my son Love, no. I mean the Idea of Love. Do you love Love?"

"I don't think your son's name is Love."

"He is love?"

"He isn't called Love."

"I am an Anglican."

"I am Catholic."

"Which means we both should not lie, Ngozika. Back to the question. Do you love the idea of Love?" He asked, "You ever been in love?"

"No."

Major Ifechukwu sat up, blinking and smiling. "You did not love your late husband?"

"I love Udoka your friend."

"That woman?" Major Ifechukwu said, wrinkling his forehead and dropping his cigarette. He had never finished a cigarette, Ngozika noticed, and he always went around with a pack or two. "That woman, Ngozika? You love a woman?"

267

"The man is a woman?"

"Yes."

Ngozika coughed, not a fake one, and said, "How? How can a man be a woman?"

"You will not understand."

"Why?"

"You are a woman."

"Women don't have brains?"

"Yes!"

Ngozika wanted to punch his face, but the fear of being killed restrained her. She got up and went to the women's toilet (where are the women? she wondered) and urinated behind the zinc house. Beside a tank, the boy Major Ifechukwu called Love was roasting the fowl. The delicious smell made Ngozika's stomach grumble, and she fought the temptation to go to the boy and beg him for meat.

It was not her intention to act weak and vulnerable, but she found herself kneeling and shaking her head gloomily. Then she was shaking and weeping. Leaves from different trees kept falling upon her unkempt hair and shoulders. When she stumbled to her feet and turned to return to Major Ifechukwu whom she found toxic, creepy, and uninteresting, she found the one she truly liked: Udoka. He was dressed in a white polo, white shorts, white boots, and his cap was white. All these were stained with soil and perhaps engine oil, but his eyes were liquid with concern and love. But what love, what kind of love? Ngozika did not know. She said, "Udoka?"

"What are you doing here, my dear?" he asked in Igbo, and she found herself hugging him. "Why are you crying here? This war is changing you. Look at how it reduced our

269

tough woman to a crying baby. Come. Come with me. I want to show you something."

Ngozika followed him to his tent. The foam was almost as flat as a mat, and it was dusty and tattered. Perhaps there were bugs in it, and it reeked of cigarettes. Udoka smoked cigarettes too? she wondered. This discovery surprised her and made her a little suspicious of the man. If he was really a smoker, why was he disinclined to enjoy one of Major Ifechukwu's several cigarettes?

"What?" he asked, looking at her with curiosity.

"What? How? What do you mean by what?"

Udoka grinned and propped his gun on a water container. "You are usually confrontational. Is the problem in you or in the war?"

"In me."

"God, she has a sense of humour. But I don't think the problem is in you. Perhaps it is in the war. No, it is obviously in the war, and not in you."

"It is in me." Ngozika picked a photograph from the foam and studied the face of the young woman. She was light-skinned and dimpled. "Your wife?"

"I promised to show you something, right?"

Ngozika brushed off a spider crawling up her hand and crushed it under her sandal. "Right."

"Guess what it is."

"I am not a kid," she said with a smile. "I have outgrown guessing games, especially this guessing game."

271

"What I want to show you is this. I want you to avoid Major Ifechukwu." He paused and looked out to see if anyone was coming. No one was coming, so he continued but in a lowered tone. "Major Ifechukwu is married to a woman. He has eight children from two different women. He has girlfriends in many towns and villages. He beats girls and married women, and I hear he rapes his wife. He will destroy you if you let him come into your life. Avoid him by all means, Ngozika."

"And come to you by all means?"

Udoka took her hand. "You have already come to me."

"What?"

"You misunderstood me. Let's go to the restaurant to find something to eat."

"You like taking me around. What does it mean?"

"It means that I am human. Am I not?"

"Major Ifechukwu is also human, isn't he?"

"No. He is a beast. Avoid him by all means."

"Don't be worried; I am not a baby. I am an adult, Udoka. Thank you."

They walked out of the tent and went to the restaurant on foot, looking away from decomposing corpses lying in the road and in bushes. And getting close to the restaurant they found boys with improvised guns, marching towards the barracks and sweating and fake-firing their weapons at the imaginary enemy that was Nigeria. They sang as they marched.

Ojukwu, we are coming to meet you

We are the true sons of the Biafra land

We are coming to see you

273

We are coming to show how willing we are

We are coming to help you tear Nigeria down

We are coming with empty hands

We are coming to beg for your help

Give us guns

Give us bombs

Give us weapons

The event must be torn into pieces like clothes

Ojukwu, the mystery air that cannot be caught, give us weapons

Guns and bombs will do the job

We are coming!

The song was in Igbo, which pleased Ngozika, and she wanted to join them but Udoka held her hand. "Please," he said. "Have you forgotten that you are a woman?"

274

"Women should not be angry? We shouldn't get angry as men?" she asked, turning to look at the group that was thinning in the distance.

"You keep misunderstanding me. Let's keep going."

"But is it true?" she asked, following him.

"What?"

"I was actually teasing. Ojukwu is coming to Umuahia. After eating, we will go to see him?"

"Sure."

"Good."

Ngozika closed her eyes as she walked and imagined her children running into her arms. Then she shook off the thoughts so that tears would not blur her vision and make

her appear weak again before this seemingly gentle man that was Udoka.

"Is there anything you would want me to do for you?" Udoka asked when they turned into the road that led to the restaurant. Fire was burning the bushes. Grey smoke curled above the trees, and kites hovered. The sky was too white to be real.

Ngozika took her eyes off the sky and said, "Yes."

"Yes?"

"Yes. Why are you so keen on helping me?"

"Is this what you would like me to do for you? Answering this very question."

"Yes. Why? I am grateful, honestly, but I am of course naturally curious. And why are

you so determined to ruin Major Ifechukwu's reputation?"

Udoka let go of her hand. "How can one ruin a reputation that has already been ruined? I repeat, he is a bad man. A terrible man. Avoid him by all means. Take my advice, Ngozika."

"Thanks."

"Now back to your first question, or was that even a question?"

"I think it was. "

Udoka opened his mouth but there was no word released; an old woman was approaching and shedding tears. "May God destroy Nigeria!" she cried. "They have killed all my children, and now they are decaying things in a stupid mass grave."

Udoka rushed to the woman to console her, and Ngozika turned and began to run

back. She knew where the mass grave was. She had passed that side on her way to receive free food from one Umuahia philanthropist who had suddenly disappeared. The place was designed for fallen Biafran people in the town, but the last time Ngozika looked at the dug ground it was free of dead bodies. Now only God knew how many corpses were thrown into the hole. Only God knew if her children were some of the dead bodies. She had not reached the place to be sure, but something told her that her children were one of the "decaying things" in the ground.

Steeling her nerves, she crept to the edge of the pit. She pushed through weeping women and children, while men stood stone-faced. Perhaps they had cried before she arrived, but it did not matter. She reached the edge and looked into the ground.

Her gaze swept over bloating bodies and flies, checking every corpse's face. I do not think my children are—her thoughts stopped. Two teen corpses were entangled at the edge of the pit. She recognized their faces, and her stomach dropped. "No. No, no!" she wailed, her knees wobbling until they could not hold her up any longer. She collapsed, her gaze never leaving her children's faces.

Nobody came to lift her.

19.

Dying to Kill

The night was a perfect stillness; there were no gunshots, bombings, screaming, or the raucous laughter that characterized Umuahia. The tents sometimes flapped and clapped when the winds were unexpectedly forceful. Lamps were out, but Ngozika knew that it would be fixed soon. Perhaps Major Ifechukwu who usually snored in his tent at night was the one doing the fixing. There was little or no kerosene here, she remembered and wondered why she was hurting her mind with this problem. She was already losing her mind. She could not wait for the sun to rise in the morning, so she could steal Udoka's machete and gun (she had lost her own) and hunt for Yorubas, Hausas, Fulanis, or any human being who identified with Nigeria.

283

"You do not love me," she said and shifted on her mat. She was not in her tent because hands like snakes usually tried to grope her boobs in the dark. I am serious, God; you do not love me. You do not love me at all. I have stopped worshipping you. I will stop praising and worshipping you because you let my two children die." She closed her mouth when she noticed a movement in the grass. A snake? A creepy creature that could sting and kill? She got up and paced up and down. Torch light flashed onto her eyes, and she stopped.

"Who be that?" asked a rough voice of a man.

"Me," Ngozika answered.

"Ngozika?"

"Yes."

The man softened in Igbo. "You have to be very careful. You scared me. No, you

disappointed me. I actually thought it was one of all these prowling wild animals. I was already salivating. You are lucky I did not pull the trigger."

She frowned but said, "Funny. Who are you, sir?"

"Forget who I am. Go back to your tent."

"Okay."

"You always forget you are a woman. You will leave soon." He turned off his torchlight and began to leave. "Do not stroll or prowl again. It's risky. It's dangerous, in fact. It is almost midnight. Be careful."

"Okay."

She returned to her tent and tried not to think about her dear children, the war, or hunger. She did not sleep until the first cockcrow, but she dreamt. In the dream, she

285

found herself carrying the bodies of her dead children, and Udoka hurried to her with tears in his eyes, and Major Ifechukwu gunned her down immediately. She jerked awake, and the morning sunlight blinded her momentarily. The cock that announced that it was morning was still crowing and she wondered why no soldier had searched for it, found it, killed, and eaten the meat in this time of hunger. She took the machete and gun lying under Major Ifechukwu's mattress and left. She would kill every Nigerian she saw.

20.

Bloody Fest

The last man Ngozika killed with her machete was a Nigerian-speaking soldier who had dropped from the back of his vehicle. They had invaded Umuahia and gunned down several Igbo people: men, children, and women. One of the pregnant women asked Ngozika to take care of her five-year-old son before she closed her eyes forever. This happened in the centre of the town and worried her that the enemy could enter into the heart of Biafra's capital and take so many lives. She joined young men and some Biafran soldiers in the bush. And as the dusty green jeep pushed its way through the deplorable road full of potholes, Ngozika threw the grenade, but it was too late; all the Nigerian soldiers had screamed and run out of the vehicle and into bushes.

The car exploded. The Biafran soldiers rushed after the fleeing enemies, and Ngozika turned sharply. Another jeep, similar in colour and size, had suddenly appeared from behind her and was coming steadily at her.

She scrambled into the bushes, using the plants to cover her. A gunshot thundered in her eardrums, and the tree beside her shook, its leaves fluttering onto her head, back, and shoulders.

The vehicle rammed into the burning one, leaving both in flames. Miraculously, she moved past this ruin without being burnt, and her clothes were unscathed. Still, the heat threatened to roast her skin. She groaned, running past leafless trees, into the heart of the bushes. In the thick brush, she ran with her hands protecting her face from thorns and

grasping twigs until she came upon a wild dog. It growled, and she ran screaming for help.

But there was no help, and the dog did not chase her.

More surprising, no Nigerian had followed her either. Despite the risks she took to bomb their cars, she was not captured. She crunched through the brush until she came to the road where she laughed. A familiar sight was scampering down this abandoned road—Mama Idu. She was hurrying in Ngozika's direction, her hair waving in the dust-laden winds, her mud-stained cream gown billowing, and no sandals covering her bleeding feet. Her friend's filthiness hurt Ngozika, but she was pleased to meet her.

When Mama Idu was close enough to hug, they embraced and sobbed. Mama Idu's clothes had been torn, and her shriveled

breasts were visible through the fabric, like a hole in her chest.

"What are you doing here?" Ngozika asked and looked back in fear.

Mama Idu turned her into a narrower road with her left hand, and said, breathing heavily, "Is this still Umuahia?"

"Yes, Umuahia, of course", Ngozika said, following her friend in a hurry as if they knew where they were going.

"I am glad that we met, Jesus!"

"What brought you here, Mama Idu? Who brought you here? It's incredible, seeing you here out of the blue. I still can't believe it's you. Who brought you here? And what happened to you? Your feet are full of blood, and your gown is torn."

"You brought me here."

"How?"

"My gown is torn? Oh, it is true! Oh Jesus! I did not know… Here, please. This road. No, this one."

Ngozika followed the grass-carpeted road Mama Idu had just indicated, the odour of dead bodies filling their nostrils "Where are we going to? Have you been here before?"

"No, I haven't. Let us keep going. I am actually on the run."

"Running from whom?"

"Danger."

"Danger?"

"Yes, Ngozika. Danger. Be faster."

"Which danger? Because I am also running from danger."

Mama Idu fell into a cluster of strange green plants, and Ngozika quickly helped her

to her feet. Mama Idu dusted her knees and said, "Thank you."

"Listen," Ngozika said and stopped.

Mama Idu spat and said, "What? What is it that? Oh, a snake?"

"No, I mean the sound. Listen. Can't you hear voices in the distance? And the sounds of cars."

"No."

"Okay, keep going. Let's keep going."

"No, Ngozika,"

"But you heard nothing, you said you heard nothing."

I heard nothing, but I am afraid. I am a coward, remember?"

"No, you are not. Coming all the way from Oguta to Umuahia is not cowardice, is it?"

"I was brought here. We were thrown into the lorry. I wanted to see you. I needed to see you. I was worried, and I missed you. It was better I died with you in Umuahia than lived in Oguta without you."

"Stop speaking like a man."

"How?"

"You have learnt to speak like a man. But I appreciate your concern, love, kindness, and new bravery. Yes, you were a coward."

"Oh, Ngozika. I wish I could laugh at the joke. The honest joke. But I am hungry, and my feet hurt."

"Let us sit on the grass."

Mama Idu looked down at the grass. "Here?"

"Yes, here. I am tired, aren't you?"

295

Mama Idu and Ngozika sat on the grass. A bird, black and white, came flying by and screeching overhead in the remarkably white sky. Surprisingly, it was late morning, almost noon, but the sun was not yet visible. The sudden sounds of gunshots tore the brief silence, and Ngozika rose.

"The Nigerian soldiers?" Mama Idu asked, her lips quivering.

"Again?"

"Yes. But I may be wrong. Those of them who captured Umuahia-- some of them, actually. They died; the others fled. But the town is not safe."

Ngozika spotted a black snake slithering in the grass, but she did not scream, did not inform her friend, but looked searchingly for a stick. She found one, behind Mama Idu, and silently, carefully, picked it up. Mama Idu

watched her with a look of mingled trepidation and curiosity. And before Mama Idu could ask Ngozika what she was up to with the stick the braver woman had smashed the head of the snake, which was about to attack.

"Jesus!" Mama Idu exclaimed.

"Forget about the snake," Ngozika said and took her friend's hand. "I hate the barracks, but we need to return there."

Mama Idu followed her with evident reluctance.

"Honestly, I ran out of the barracks. I was told you were there. I went there to see you, but I could not meet you.

"Who did you meet? How did you get there?"

"It is a long story. I met a soldier called Udoka. Soft like a girl, and not like a soldier.

I gave him some of your Ernest Hemingway novels, but he was killed. He was telling— no, advising me—to avoid Major General Ifechukwu, but the beast overhead him and gunned him down. This beast had been raping me. I escaped from him, and here we are. Udoka also told me that it was Major Ifechukwu who forced your children and other children into the army – and they were killed."

They were now on the road. Ngozika could not believe what she had heard. Her heart was beating so fast. The world appeared blurry in her eyes, and her feet were shaky with fury. She coughed and implored Mama Idu to repeat what she had just said, and her friend obliged.

Then, again, the world began to go blurry as though the eyes viewing it belonged to a

drunk, but Ngozika could not remember the last time she tasted alcohol. No, she thought. No, she could remember, and it was palm wine two or three months ago, and it was with the "beast" Major Ifechukwu, and he had tried to force her to sleep with him afterwards. It was Udoka who saved her by screaming that a snake had entered into the barracks, near the tent, and they—Major Ifechukwu and Ngozika—had jumped off the bench and their glasses fell and shattered. Now Udoka, according to Mama Idu who was popular with her honesty (and cowardice) had died. It was Major Ifechukwu, and not the gentle and kind Udoka and not Ngozika's children, that should have died.

"Let's go to the barracks, Mama Idu," she said.

"Why? Why, please?" Mama Idu asked in English. "Let's go."

"They will kill us if we—"

"Let's go. You will wait near Udoka's popular restaurant for me."

"What do you want to do there at the barracks, Ngo?"

"We both know, and I will succeed. Kindly wait at the restaurant. I will meet you ten or fifteen minutes later. No further questions, please." Ngozika reached for the knife in her belt that she had carried since the soldier gave it to her.

When Ngozika arrived in the barracks, the sun had appeared in the sky, and Major Ifechukwu and six soldiers, all men, were all playing football with the head of a Hausa man they had killed. Major Ifechukwu told her it was the head of a Hausa man after they had entered into his office—a zinc square the size of a tank. She was naked and sweating, but Major Ifechukwu was not in a hurry to do to her what he had been longing to do to her. He said, "Why are you suddenly naked? It's strange. But your breasts are beautiful."

"Thank you," she said, her eyes on his desk. A knife, peeled oranges, partially eaten oranges, packs of cigarettes all littered the furniture.

"Let me guess," he said, going to close the door.

"You came back to see Udoka, your secret lover."

"No."

"Yes."

"No."

"Don't lie; I am not jealous. He was nicer and more handsome."

"But you are braver."

"You don't want to ask me how he died. Who told you about his passing?" He came to her and grabbed her breast. Slapping his hand away, she pushed him and made for the knife on the table. The major staggered backwards to knock open the door he had closed with his back when Ngozika rushed at him. He would not allow her near the table, so she reached for the knife on her belt.

She buried that knife into his chest, ducking to avoid the spray of blood that gushed out. Major Ifechukwu screamed and dropped like a brick. She climbed the cupboard and escaped through the open window.

Sounds of hurried footsteps and curious soldiers rushed into the room, but by then she

was close to the fence. Gunshots fired after her. As her heartbeat thundered, she ran at the fence, scaling it and lifting herself over and across to meet Mama Idu.

21.

Riding to the End on Troubled Waters

"**O**h God, you did?" Mama Idu asked.

"Yes."

"How? How did you do that? No one caught you?"

"I am glad that I killed him," Ngozika told Mama Idu and then narrated the heroic encounter with Major Ifechukwu in the barracks.

"Oh, my God," Mama Idu said, her eyes dilated as though she had not known that Ngozika was going to murder Major Ifechukwu, as though she did not see in Ngozika's heavy breathing as they ran to this place, the untold story of a killing.

Ngozika had found some drying clothes to cover her naked body, but she cleaned the

307

blood on her hands and face as they ran. They had escaped from Umuahia and were not in a strange town not far away. But what was the name of the town? Ngozika did not know. She did not even want to know.

"Where are we running to?" Mama Idu asked, panting behind Ngozika. Their sandals were covered with dirt, and their clothes were soaked with sweat.

"I don't know," Ngozika answered. "But I want us to run as far as we can. If possible, let's leave Igbo land. Not possible, I admit, but we can try."

"I am hungry."

"As always."

"As always?"

Ngozika apologized, and they continued running. She did not provoke her confused friend any longer until they arrived in a bushy village in this strange town. They did not know where they were; they could not read the signboards written in strange Igbo, they could not speak the dialect, and they could not venture back to Oguta because the soldiers would capture her, and that would be the end of her life. Perhaps her punishment would not be stoning, not burning alive, not throwing her into the Ogbuide River, but burying her alive in the barracks' cell where, as she heard, the sun never shone.

A group of three thin middle-aged women ambling down a tree-lined path riveted their attention. On these women's heads and on their shoulders: empty buckets. One of them walked with two little girls, identical twins of seven or eight, and they, like their mother, like their mother's companions, carried buckets. Obviously, Ngozika thought,

they are journeying to a river to collect water for the day.

"Call me Exhausted, darling," Mama Idu said, searching the sky for the moon that had already set. The sun would be rising soon. "Call me Hungry. Call me Dead."

"Call me Hope," Ngozika said in her shaky voice and clutched Mama Idu's hand. "We're going to the river with them. If we become their friends, we may live in their house until we decide what to do, where to go, and how to escape from Igbo land until the war is truly over–"

Ngozika knew that Mama Idu did not catch all her words because the wind, dust-laden and howling, came with unexpected ferocity and blew off her words and her hat. The dry leaves on the road flew up into the sky of enamelled blue, mingled with the purple

feathers fanning out from the wings of ear-splittingly noisy birds in flight, and began to descend, slowly, teasingly, with some clouds of dust. A tree collapsed behind them, someone screamed down the road, and Ngozika and Mama Idu started to run towards the women with buckets. They ran past whispering trees, past herds of cattle, past a tornado of whirlwinds, past weary palm wine tappers on their way out with their cans of palm wine. This continued until they caught sight of the three women with buckets who, like them, were also running towards the rising sun, which was now a shining orange climbing into the green branches of swaying trees on a green mountain.

They all ended up at the bank of a river, whose waters had been transformed to the colour of tea by the fallen branches of termite-filled trees. This river was free of human

lives, except for two white-haired fishermen whistling poignant tunes of bereavement in a boat. They paddled to the shore and anchored their boat on the trunk of a leafless but sturdy tree whose name Ngozika had forgotten. They seemed to be in a hurry, these men, because they waved hurriedly, and there was no verbal greeting, no wide-eyed inspection, no sexual objectification, and commenced a hasty ascent on the deserted road. The women with buckets and twin sisters looked from the retreating figures of the fishermen to the two friends on the run and to the river which had, miraculously, returned to its serene colourlesssness, as fishes jumped and the waters clapped.

"Danger lurks," Mama Idu said in a voice free of anxiety. "Oh, that hill!"

Ngozika, together with the women, the sisters, followed her pointing fingers to the mountain where an animal shaped like a lion prowled. A lion, really, or a tiger, or a dog, or a wolf? Ngozika did not know, and as she turned to scream, the women with the buckets screamed.

Mama Idu dashed to the departed fishermen's boat and pulled at the rusted chain that was used to anchor it to the tree. And thankfully, a machete, rusty but strong, was buried in the tree trunk. She pulled it aggressively, like a warrior that she was, and cut the chain at once. The women, the girls, and Ngozika flew into the boat with synchronous yells of mingled excitement and trepidation. And the waters, disturbed by their anxious feet, splashed violently at the trunk, poured liberally on the grasses of marvelous green and yellow and silver, and a frog leapt out and into pink flowers being combed perpetually by the rising winds from the south.

She paddled the boat, Mama Idu and the women applauded. The girls sang of their father, sang of their father's father, sang of their father's mother: in distinct but astonishingly ponderable Igbo, which was, to Ngozika, inferior to the unsurpassingly lyrical dialect spoken in Oguta.

The plaintive melodiousness of the girls' voices put tears in Ngozika's eyes, but she wiped them with her palm, the waters grumbling as though ghosts were quarrelling under the boat. "Where are we going?" Ngozika asked in a quavering voice, and the winds snatched the words and threw them behind them.

"Across the river?" the thinnest one answered. "We will stay there until men capture the animal and kill it. We heard some lions escaped from a zoo uptown, but we did not believe it. Now, see!"

"Your names?" Mama Idu asked, paddling faster, and Ngozika was quite surprised by this unexpected show of bravery. "Mine is Mama Idu. Call me Idu. Just Idu, for a reason."

The name caused the women's eyebrows to go up in undisguised amazement. Obviously, Ngozika thought, they had mistaken Mama Idu for a man, and Idu, in every Oguta village, in every Igbo land, is a male name, and not for women, and for Mama Idu to take the name, it meant she was a woman despite her uncharacteristic bravery, despite her broad shoulders, despite her deep voice.

"But you're a man?" one of the girls asked, blinking as the winds, now heavy with chilly waters, rushed into her innocent face.

"Mummy, isn't she a woman? She acts like a man."

"No, she's a manly woman, or maybe a man, yes," her mother answered, and screamed at a jumping fish. It jumped one more time and sank into the waters now painted gorgeous red, like spilled blood and oil, by the rising sun. At their right-hand side, across the river, there are rocks of gigantic sizes from which blue-coloured water raged and gushed and flowed into the river to get muddled with redness. Billowing leaves dropped into the waters, into the boat, into the mouths of the sisters who had resumed their poignant singing, and a booming thunder, and blinding lightning, began, almost simultaneously, to prevail. The river, now tenanted by the glassy brilliance of the menacingly persistent lightning, began to growl and splash and threaten to capsize the boat. The women yelped— and Ngozika did likewise. The girls, singing and weeping, looked skyward as if they were in search of the face of the Merciful God.

They sang, prayed, and cried until the clouds opened, and rain pummeled the boat. Shivering, they yelled and gasped as the rain raged, slapping their faces and pushing the boat ferociously forward.

"Mummy, are we going to drown?" the same girl asked.

"No!" the three women bawled in perturbed intonations and gazed at heaven. The twins started scooping the rainwater out of the boat with their hands.

"We only came to fetch water," the thinnest woman said, and the wind snatched her lavender scarf and tossed it across the waters. "God, save us…!"

The winds, mounting in intensity, engulfed some of her words, and thunder boomed. The kids shrieked as though they were needled by the devil. The boat continued to sail until leaf-filled waters, rushing frothily from another river, flooded theirs and tilted their boat, splashing into their faces and baskets and boat. Someone screamed the name of Jehovah Jireh – one of the girls, perhaps – and the boat shook and rocked and turned.

The waters, carrying a drowned baby with no head and no arms, attacked the boat, pushing it dangerously backward, sending it bouncing implausibly back to the frothy channel they had been following, and the twins dropped off and into the waters with their buckets. In helpless silence, Ngozika watched them scream for their screaming mother to rescue them.

Ngozika watched the waters assail their faces, throw them up, as if to send them back into the boat, submerge them, throw them up once more, and finally, heartbreakingly, swallow them like a shark. Unreasonable with sorrow and panic, the inconsolably screaming mother of the girls flew off the boat like some mad bird into the waters, which threw her up, as it had thrown her kids, and then swallowed her whole.

As Ngozika cried, Mama Idu paddled, frantically, clumsily, hopelessly, and thunder continued to boom and threaten to strike somebody. And the lightning, too. From time to time, it brightened their faces, the lightening, and lit the surface of the waters like a fluorescent light put in a pure glass. The grumbling clouds crowded so suddenly to cover the rising sun.

Ngozika glanced over her shaking shoulders and found the bodies of the women and the girls, upturned, afloat, following the boat as if, though lifeless, they were desirous to see how this turbulent voyage would end. Their surviving friend suddenly emitted a savage cry of agony. The currents, seemingly mingled with crystalized waters that instantaneously brought icebergs and sea to Ngozika's laborious mind, hit the boat with heightened aggressiveness, not once, not twice, not thrice, like a provoked bull, and Ngozika saw the woman tumble into the roaring mouth of the waters.

Mama Idu instinctively abandoned her paddles and dived into the water to rescue her. Ngozika stood and yowled before sitting, shaking. She was shaking because Mama Idu could not be glimpsed: the rain had become incredibly furious. She felt like a drenched pigeon encased in an opaque tank made of glass as the boat, ignorant of her fate and its fate, and continued to travel drunkenly. When the rain softened, the powdery world became a little clearer. She gazed back again but beheld neither the drowned women nor the drowned girls, nor the possibly drowned prospective rescuer. To her surprise, she did not cry, did not feel the need to jump off the boat and join the floating bodies, but began to sing *"It's well with my soul…"*

She shivered as she sang, and the rain, miraculously, slowed to a drizzle. But the winds were colder – freezing, in fact – and most of her mournful words were engulfed by the invisible, whizzing hands of these winds. Yet she continued to sing of Hosanna in the Highest. She sang, clapped, and cried; and the boat, now hers alone, shuddered as if it, too, had caught cold. Again, she resumed, tearfully, scooping the rainwater filling the boat. She did this as she sang praises to God for the little but memorable time she spent with Mama Idu on earth. The waters, producing resonant sounds resembling the hymns sung by some choir rehearsing in an empty cathedral, carried the boat down the river and towards the rainbows, which had now graced the sky.

Ngozika counted the colours, like a character in a low-budget movie, to make certain they were seven. Then she closed her eyes, thanking Jehovah, praising Jehovah, welcoming Jehovah, as rainwater trickled down her cheeks, as her teeth chattered in the cold. The boat continued to float on the troubled waters. Then she saw with horror that the boat was returning her to the land from which she had just escaped.

And perhaps the soldiers were there waiting for her. Waiting to catch her, slaughter, and throw her corpse to dogs. She would not give them that opportunity. Only God knew what they were saying.

Was Ernest Hemingway thinking about his enemy when he pulled the trigger? Only God knew. She took the knife from her belt. There is no place for a woman of Biafra among soldiers and guns, Ngozika thought. My children are dead, and my best friend is gone. Soon, I will be gone. Pulling back her arm, she plunged the knife into her chest. A scream escaped, though it gurgled with the last of her breath, and blood gushed into the boat. She slumped with her eyes wide open, and the boat continued to float on the blood-stained water.

Acknowledgements

I am grateful to Ebelenna Esomnofu, Ikenna Okeh and R. Ramey-Guerrero, my first readers. For the thorough editing and delicate notes. I am grateful.

Katalin Mund, my agent, for her tireless effort.

Thanks to Abraham Aondoana. Thank you, George K. George.

David Hundeyin, thank you very much for all your support.

I am indebted to Charles Akwari, for the financial support that helped this come through and Kene Anosike, who purchased many copies even before it was published.

Arinze Ezieke, Mishael Maro Amos, Yemi Edun, Iyinoluwa Aboyeji, Kelvin Kellman, James Egwuenu, Terry Odenigbo, Ramesh Raparthy, Bobby Combz, Adeleke Togun, Jide Sowemimo, Chike Odigie, Chudie Igweonu, Nzube Olikeze and everyone supporting me.

Obiora Anozie, my great friend, who stands solidly behind me.

Dr. Sabine Jell-Bahlsen for all the lessons. Grateful to Dr. Shola Adenekan, for all the love.

Blessing Onerije, thank you for support. And you, Tochi Nwokeafor.

Debbie Edwards, my manager, Eternally grateful.

Dinesh Chakravarthy, my publisher at Abibiman Publishing India. For everything.

My siblings, Chijioke, Odinaka, Nkechi, Ebere and Ifeanyi. I am lucky to have you all.

Mr. Jahman Anikulapo, thank you for all your support.

Olamma Agwu Kalu, my dearest, for taking the time to proof-read.

Godswill Ugwuamaka, the friend anyone would dream of. Thank you for your constant support.

Professor Lesyle Obiora, Nkechi Obiora and Noel Obiora, the best family anyone would dream of. Thank you for holding it down for me.

Mrs Weruche Emeruem, my cheerleader. For calling to check up on me every day. I love you.

Finally, to Professor Wole Soyinka and Professor Akachi Ezeigbo. Thank you!